The redhead gives [illegible] wriggle and her eyes meet mine.
'Could you pass me [illegible] puts the toast
back on the plate a[illegible]
with breakfast in b[illegible]
everywhere and st[illegible]
I pass her the tiss[illegible] on
it. I have never se[illegible] as
if it has somethin[illegible] er if
you had a go?' And, so [illegible]
her boobs and pulls them apart, doesn't she? [illegible] d?'

Also by Timothy Lea

CONFESSIONS OF A POP PERFORMER
CONFESSIONS FROM A HEALTH FARM
CONFESSIONS FROM THE SHOP FLOOR
CONFESSIONS OF A LONG DISTANCE LORRY DRIVER
CONFESSIONS OF A PLUMBER'S MATE
CONFESSIONS OF A PRIVATE DICK

Timothy Lea

Confessions from a Luxury Liner

Futura Publications Limited

A Futura Book

First published in Great Britain in 1976
by Futura Publications Limited

ISBN 0 8600 7298 3

Printed in Great Britain by
Hazell Watson & Viney Ltd
Aylesbury, Bucks

Futura Publications Limited
Warner Road, London SE5

CONTENTS

CHAPTER ONE

In which Timmy reveals a terpsichorean talent and spends an energetic evening in the company of brother-in-law, Sid, and fun-loving Gloria and Natalie.

'Was it nice, Sid?' I ask.

Clapham's answer to Paul Newman grits his Teds like he has plans to make them retractable. 'Watch it!' he hisses. 'Just watch it. I'm not telling you again.'

Readers of *Confessions of a Private Dick* will recall that my brother-in-law and partner, Sidney Noggett, ran into a spot of bother at the end of our career as C Men working for Mission E – or Emission as it was widely known in concentric circles at the Ministry of Defence. I will not spoil the story for those who have not read it by revealing the amazing details, but suffice to say that Sid's distress was occasioned by an unsolicited sexual encounter – and there are not many of those flying around as far as Mrs Noggett's little boy is concerned, I don't mind telling you. Sid usually holds back from nooky the way a freshly sharpened hatchet rests lightly on half a pound of warm butter.

'I'm not asking for the unpleasant details,' I say.

'Don't ask for anything,' says Sid. 'Otherwise your lower lip is going to look like Iddy Amin's pyjama case. Anyway, what have you got to rabbit about? You haven't heard from your precious Retchen, have you?'

'Gretchen,' I grit.

'No doubt some horny Kraut is introducing her to his Frankfurter at this very moment,' says Sid, clearly warming to the idea. 'Oh yes, I reckon you can say "auf wiedersehen" to that little number.'

I try to look as if the idea is too blooming stupid to comment on but in my heart of hearts I fear that he may well be right. Gretchen went back to Germany three weeks ago and I have not heard a dicky bird since. Our bitter-sweet romance was not helped when the local anaesthetic I used to assist in its consummation sent my dick to sleep half a second after penetration. I would have cried if Gretchen had not beaten me to it. It was all so sad because she went home before I had the chance to introduce her to the full lustre of my cluster.

'She'll write,' I say. 'Don't you worry.'

'I'm not worried,' says Sid. 'Not about that, anyway. Of all the bleeding things I've got to worry about, your bit of Hun fluff is very low on the list.' He takes a long sip of Mum's tea and his face wrinkles in disgust. 'Gordon Bennett! Can't your Mum even make a cup of tea? Look at the brown rings round the inside of this cup. They've eaten into the china.'

'Mum puts something with it to make it go further,' I tell him.

'*This* isn't going to go any further,' says Sid pushing his cup away. 'Blimey, I wish I'd brought my clogged-up paint brushes with me. Stick 'em in this lot for a few minutes and you could paint the Mona Lisa with them.'

Sid and I are having a cuppa round at 17 Scraggs Lane, the ancestral home of the Leas, and we are supposed to be discussing our future. No sooner has my brother-in-law emptied the contents of his cup down the sink than my mother enters clutching a couple of letters.

'I didn't know people still wrote letters,' says Sid. 'Still, when it's a choice between spending the money on a stamp or a few hundred British Leyland shares . . .'

'There's one from Germany,' says Mum. 'Quite a pretty stamp. You wouldn't think the Germans would have a stamp like that.'

'Here it comes,' says Sid cheerfully. 'The old brush-off, Kraut-style. Get your handkerchief out.'

'Oh look,' says Mum. 'Somebody's poured their tea leaves into the sink. What a waste. You can dry them and use them again mixed with dandelion leaves. I heard it on the wireless.'

'That was for pipe tobacco, not drinking!' says Sid. 'No wonder it tasted so diabolical. That bleeding tom is always up against the dandelions.'

My finger and thumb are testing the contents of the air-mail envelope. It does not seem over-thick for a passionate love letter. Perhaps I would be better off reading it in the privacy of my own very small room.

'Read us out the fruity bits,' says Sid. He snatches the envelope and holds it under his hooter. 'Phew! Eau de Sauerkraut. She must have been off with some bloke when she posted this.'

'She was a nice enough girl,' says Mum. 'For a foreigner, that is.'

'I know, Mum,' I say. 'Their ways are not our ways, are they?'

'That's exactly what I always say,' says Mum.

'I know it is,' I say wearily.

'He's taking the piss,' says Sid. 'I think love has coarsened him.'

'That's not nice,' says Mum.

I suppress a sigh and tear open the envelope. I do wish Sid would spend a bit more time in his trendy Vauxhall pad with my sister Rosie and his two delightful children, Jason and Dominic. He always said how much he loathed

Scraggs Lane when he was forced to live here. Now he never stops hanging about the place.

'Dear Timmy,' I read. 'I hope you are well. I am sorry I am not writing more soon but there is very much happening when I arrive home. I have seen many old faces. One of them is Horst. I do not remember if I tell you around him. He is maybe the reason why I leave home. He has told me that he misses me very much and I think that I miss him, too. At Christmas we become engaged so I will not be coming back to England.'

I let the letter drop to waist level and Sid does not have to go to night school to read my expression. 'Like I said, eh?' he says cheerfully. 'The big elbow. You can't say I didn't warn you.'

'Thanks,' I say.

'Is there someone else?' says Mum. She sounds quite perky, too. Of course, she was never keen on me marrying a daughter of the Third Reich, desperate as she was for me to get spliced to someone.

'Seems like it,' I say.

'Oh well,' says Mum. 'I expect it's for the best. You never met her people, did you?'

'They were Nazi war criminals,' I say. 'I saw her Dad on Colditz the other night.'

I try and entertain myself by imagining a wedding photograph of Mum standing next to a geezer wearing jack boots, monocle, sabre scars and Iron Cross, but the ache still hangs round my stomach like suet round a kidney. I think that you only really care for a bird when she gives you the boot.

'You wouldn't have had anything to live on,' says Mum. 'There's that to be thankful for.'

I think I know what Mum means. Sid and I are indeed

skint since we parted company with Mission E and the queue at the National Assistance counter grows longer daily.

'Yes, he's well out of that, there's no doubt about it,' says Sid. 'She doesn't know how lucky she is, either. Still, that's all water that's been passed under the bridge. We've got to turn our minds to thoughts of the future. Talent like ours is too precious to lie mouldering on the shelf.'

'It's not easy to get a job these days,' says Mum. 'They're laying off more people than they're laying on them.'

'You don't lay on people, Mum,' I say.

'No, but you do,' says Sid. Sid has what might be described as a very personal sense of humour. He is the only person to laugh at his jokes.

Mum waits for him to finish. 'Look what happened to your father,' she sniffs. 'They nearly made him red-redundant.'

This is indeed true. Dad's position at the lost property office – slumped over a desk in a posture resembling deep kip – was only preserved by the fact that a lot of people suddenly lost a lot of things and he was able to prove that London would grind to a halt without him. The situation was so desperate that he was actually taking stuff that he had nicked back to the office.

'They should have kicked him out years ago,' says Sid. 'Spongers like him are the reason why this once great country of ours is in the mess it is now. The lazy old git has never done a day's work in his life and he's pocketing God knows how much money every week as well as all the stuff he swipes.'

'That's not a nice way to talk about your father-in-law,' says Mum.

'No, but it's true,' says Sid. 'It makes me sick when I

think how I've embodied the very spirit of Britain's merchant greatness and ended up without a penny piece to show for it. Look at the businesses I've started, look at the initiative and dynamism I've demonstrated, look at the employment I've offered.'

'Look at the wages you haven't paid,' I say. 'I'm your most regular employee and I've hardly made a couple of quid in four years.'

'You're a chip off the old block and no mistake,' says Sid. 'Just like your old Dad. Grasping and ungrateful. You've had the opportunity to learn more with me than you would in a dozen business schools, but all you can think about is money. You embody everything that is wrong with this country. Frankly, I've had enough. I feel that Britain has betrayed me. There's no place here any more for a man with ideals, courage and untamable ambition. I've thought about it long and hard in the last few days, Timmo, and I've decided that there is only one thing to do.'

'Emigrate, Sid?' I say.

'Don't be stupid,' says Sid. 'I don't want to chuck away the National Health and the assistance – God knows, I've earned it. I was thinking of working out of the country for a bit.'

'The Isle of Wight,' says Mum. 'That's where I've always wanted to go. The climate is very like our own. I don't like it too hot.'

'Somewhere slightly further afield is what I had in mind,' says Sid. 'I was thinking of blazing the ocean's trails in the merchant marine.'

'Oh,' says Mum. 'That sounds nice. What did you have in mind exactly?'

'A ship's steward,' says Sid. 'I was talking to somebody

the other night and they made it sound a wonderful job. You meet a lot of interesting people and travel all round the world. It would be like a holiday after what we've been through lately.'

'What about Rosie?' says Mum.

'She'll be all right,' says Sid. 'She's got her business interests to look after and – you know what they say – absence makes the heart grow fonder.'

'Like me and Gretchen,' I say.

Sid does not savour the flavour of that remark and it is necessary for me to invest in a pint of pig's at the Nightingale before he starts to get back to something like his normal self. 'Wouldn't break you to buy a packet of crisps, would it?' he says.

'It would as a matter of fact,' I say. 'What do you want?'

'Cheese and onion,' he says. 'And make sure they're not soggy.'

'How do you reckon I do that?' I say. 'Grind them to powder between my fingers before I cough up the cash?'

'I'll leave it to you,' he says. 'I just can't bear it when you can bend them.'

Two minutes later I give him a packet of Oxo flavoured crisps with the explanation that the boozer has run out of cheese and onion.

'You know I can't stand those,' he says. 'And where's the packet of salt? They've started doing the salt again, you know.'

'Maybe it's a different make,' I say. 'No, wait a minute, it can't be. I've got three packets in mine.'

'Typical,' says Sid. 'I even miss out when it comes to the bleeding salt.' He looks at my crisps. 'Hey! I thought you said they'd run out of cheese and onion.'

'They have,' I say. 'I got the last packet.'

'That's disgusting!' says Sid. 'Haven't you got no manners? Your side of the family are so uncouth.'

'You can't talk about being uncouth,' I say. 'Look at all those little bits of crisp floating on top of your beer. It quite puts me off my food.'

'Good,' says Sid. 'Then you won't need your crisps.' And he grabs my packet and shoves half of it down his cakehole.

Fortunately, that half includes two of the packets of salt as the bloke next door soon finds out when Sid spits them into an ashtray and covers his whistle in ash.

'I don't know what he was making so much bleeding fuss about,' says Sid as we hurry through the door. 'It was a grey suit. A bit of ash is good for them.'

'Not when it covers up the pin stripe,' I say. 'Where are we going to go now, the Highwayman?'

'No,' says Sid. 'I'm nipping up to the Palais. Do you want to come?'

'The Palais?' I say. 'I haven't been there for years. I didn't know you were into dancing.'

'I'm not, am I?' says Sid. 'I've got a date with this bird who might be able to help us with the steward thing. Her old man is on the turn—' at least, that is what I think he says. It is not until I have expressed sympathy that I learn that the lady's husband serves on a boat called the *Tern*.

'What do you need me for?' I say.

'She's certain to have a friend,' says Sid. 'They always do, don't they? You can look after her while I sort out Gloria.'

'She goes there a lot while her old man's at sea, does she?' I ask.

'She gets lonely,' says Sid. 'You can understand it. Everybody needs a bit of company, don't they?'

'Is that where you met her?' I ask.

'No,' says Sid. 'She was in The Highwayman on Friday night. She goes up there for the charity draw.'

'Sounds very public spirited,' I say. 'You giving her one, are you?'

'You don't ask people questions like that when they're happily married,' says Sid. 'Bugger! I forgot to buy any peppermints when I was in the boozer.'

I am not over thrilled about going up the Palais because it is not cheap and I can't dance to keep my joints from seizing up. I took a postal course once but it never showed you how to marry the footprints up to the music and you don't like to ask your partner when to start and what sort of dance it is, do you? It is also a bit imitation posh and I don't go a bundle on that either. You have to wear a tie in the Princess Bar and there is a Brylcreem dispenser in the gents – or 'Caballeros' as it is called.

'Aren't we going to have a few beers first?' I say. 'It never tastes the same with a carpet under your feet.'

'Stop moaning,' says Sid. 'If we could get a job on one of these boats we could be putting ourselves in line for a new world of experiences. Gloria will be able to tell us all about it.'

'We'd be better off with her old man, wouldn't we?'

'I hope not,' says Sid. 'Anyway, he's chugging round the Mediterranean, lucky bastard.' He squirts an aerosol spray round the inside of the Rover and it is clear the way his mind is working. The Alsatian is the back window will have something to nod about before the night is out.

The Palais does not seem to have changed much from when I last saw it. Maybe the manager has a little more scar tissue round his mince pies than when I last saw him but it is difficult to be certain. He looks just as suspicious and worried as he did in the old days. Sid starts to hum 'I'm putting on my white tie' as he fumbles for his wallet, and my stomach heaves. I have a distant recollection of Rosie's wedding when they piled the metal chairs on top of each other in the church hall, poured sand from the fire buckets over the pools of sick and danced until the Brownies rolled up. Sid had quite a dazzling quarter turn in those days I seem to remember. And something called the fish tail that involved hopping across the floor as if it was white hot coals and somebody had dropped a jellyfish down your Y-fronts.

I am just about to suggest that Sid might like to buy me the other half when he stiffens and squares his enormous shoulders. It is obvious that somewhere amongst the crispy noodle of lacquered barnet he has spotted Gloria.

'Right, here we go,' he breathes. 'Try and match my mood of breathless suavity. She likes a laugh so cheer yourself up a bit. You look like you dropped fifty pence in a dog turd.'

'Is it true that Laurence Olivier is playing you in *The Sid Noggett Story*?' I ask.

Sid does not reply because he has already fixed a horrible smile on his gnashers and is gliding forward full of wild animal magic. I follow a few paces behind him, checking on the position of the exit doors. He is steering for a couple of blondes and from behind they do not look bad. The hair colour comes straight out of a bottle but the rest of them seems natural enough. Only time and the subtle pressure of my sensitive germans will tell.

'Sid!' One of the birds has turned round and her face actually lights up. This is quite something at the Palais where it is cool to treat everyone like you are only just too good mannered to tell them that they have terminal BO.

'Hidy hi! How are we then? Looking pretty fantastic, I must say.' Sid takes both her mits in his and holds her at arm's length like the two of them were left over when the screen went blank after an old Doris Day movie.

'You're not looking so bad yourself, is he Natalie?'

Natalie might be Gloria's sister and she nods and giggles. Then everyone looks at me. Sid is wearing his fawn denim Sanders of the river safari suit, and both the birds have shiny dresses, so I suppose I am what you might call a bit underdressed. Certainly, Joe Bugner's sparring partner in the dinner jacket on the door gave me an old-fashioned look. Sid swiftly gauges that the female reaction to me is not exactly white hot.

'This is my kid brother-in-law, Timmy,' he says. 'He's saving up for a suit.'

'A paternity suit,' I say. I reckon this is quite quick and verging on the amusing but neither of the birds seem to coco it overmuch. They are too busy running their eyes over my threads like they wish they were vacuum cleaners. I have to admit that my Chinese tank top from 'Gone Wong' in the High Street was a bit of a mistake and someone ought to tell the chinks that we are not all built like spaghetti with shoulder blades. Still, the Judies are clocking me from the best side because it is only when you are standing behind me that you can see where all the seams have gone.

'Pleased to meet you,' says Gloria without sounding as if she means it.

'Hello,' says Natalie with less enthusiasm than Gloria.

'Great!' says Sid, rubbing his hands together. 'How would you girls fancy a drink?'

'In a glass,' says Gloria.

'Oh yes, very good,' says Sid trying to strike a few

sparks off my glazed eyeballs. 'We've got a couple of bright ones here, Timmo.'

'Definitely,' I say, trying desperately to work a little enthusiasm into my voice. 'What would you like, girls?'

'Pernod,' says Gloria.

'Pernod,' says Natalie.

'That's a kind of absinthe, isn't it?' says Sid.

'That's right,' I say. 'You know what they say. "Absinthe makes the heart grow fonder".'

Of course, I am wasting my time weaving dizzy verbal patterns round these birds who would probably have difficulty arranging 'off piss' into a well known phrase or saying, and I need my head examined trying a second attempt at humour when the first has been a disaster. If a bird starts off finding you funny, that is great, but if you are up against the strong silent type you might as well forget it. Gloria and Natalie look at me as if I have caused them physical pain and Sid winces.

'What's the matter with you?' he says as he elbows me up against the bar. 'Are you trying to make them think you're some kind of nutter? If you can't say anything sensible, belt up. I'd better go and set their minds at ease. I'll have a scotch.' And with that, he is gone. Lea gets lumbered with the drinks again. I can see them all looking at me. Sid is saying something and the two birds are leaning forward like he is describing the first symptoms of rabies.

'That'll be two pounds thirty pence, mate.'

'Two pounds thirty pence!'

'This is the doubles bar.'

I pay up and stagger over to where Sid is sitting, determined to see a return on my investment. The last time I laid out this kind of money on a bird I thought she was buying her trousseau with it.

'Haven't they got any ice?' says Gloria.

'I'd like some water with mine,' says Natalie.

Marvellous, isn't it? You would think my jeans would be sodden with tears of gratitude after all the moola I have lashed out. Instead of that they treat me as if I am a blooming butler.

'Come on, Timmo,' says Sid. 'Get it together. See if you can find some nuts while you're about it.'

'I think I know where I can find a couple straight off.' I say.

I leave him to think about it and pad back to the bar. The plastic pumpkin is full of lukewarm water and dead flies, and when I mention ice the barman looks at me as if I have asked for the kiss of life. 'It's finished, mate,' he says. 'People take it.'

'That's terrible,' I say, realising immediately that sarcasm is wasted on him. 'Is there anywhere here I can get some?'

'You might try the Orchestra Bar,' he says. 'They don't have the same run on it down there.'

So I pour the water from the plastic pumpkin into a glass, fish out the flies, and take it back to the girls. Natalie does not even say ta but pours it straight into her Pernod.

'Oh look,' I say. 'It's turned cloudy. Do you want me to take it back?'

'It's supposed to do that, you twit!' hisses Sid. 'Piss off and find some ice.'

So I am across the dance floor like a ball of mercury and amazed to find that the plastic pumpkin on the counter of the Orchestra Bar is full of ice. I snatch it up and have taken one step back the way I came when the geezer behind the bar buries his voice in my earhole.

'Here! Where do you think you're going?' he says.

'I want some ice,' I say.

'Well, you can't take that,' he says.

'Listen,' I say. 'Don't give me a bad time. My patience is becoming exhausted. I'm not nicking your bleeding pumpkin for a kiddy's piss pot. I just want some ice for a couple of drinks.'

'I don't care if you want it to embalm your pet lizard,' says the bloke. 'You're not taking that tub.'

As it turns out, the bloke is right. I take another couple of purposeful strides and the ice bucket is jerked out of my hands as if it is attached to a chain fastened to the counter – which it is. A shower of iced balls fly across the floor and four couples fall arse over tit in the middle of their ladies' excuse me. I am fortunate to be able to pick up half a dozen balls and lose myself in the confusion. When I get back to Sid and the girls, my hands are dripping and the balls have nearly disappeared – I gave them a quick suck in case they had picked up any dirt, which did not help. After all my efforts, I am not overthrilled to find that the birds have finished their drinks.

'That's great,' I say. 'I've got six balls and you don't want any of them.'

'Stop lying and being disgusting,' says Sid. 'You must learn to judge when you're giving offence.' He turns to Gloria. 'Would you care to take the floor?'

'Watch him,' I say. 'He won't even help you carry it out to the lorry.'

I know what I said a few paragraphs ago but sometimes you don't care, do you? Sid goes past me with a look of disdain illuminating his noble features and soon he and Gloria are dancing their way into the record books. That leaves me with Natalie and my bus fare home. It is for this latter reason that I ignore her blood red fingernails toying with the stem of her empty glass.

'I believe Gloria's husband is afloat?' I say, revealing that easy gift for conversation that makes it so amazing that I am one of the few people in the country who has never appeared on the Michael Parkinson Show.

Natalie looks puzzled. 'A what?' she says. 'He's English.'

I think hard and realise that there has been a misunderstanding. 'No,' I say with a light laugh. 'I mean, he is a seafaring man, a jolly jack tar, "fifteen men on a dead man's chest" and all that kind of thing.' I lean forward and give her my Robert Newton. ' "Them as dies 'll be the lucky ones. Aaaargh, Jim boy. Aaaargh!" ' Natalie draws back and looks around nervously. Maybe I should have gone a bit easy on the eyeball rolling. Still, you see worse on children's television. Much worse.

It is not something that I particularly care to be seen doing in public but it occurs to me that in the present situation there is probably no way out. 'Do you fancy a—?' I say, jerking my head towards the dance floor.

Natalie closes her eyes momentarily as if racked by a sharp pang of toothache. 'All right,' she says.

Like I have said before, my dancing is lousy but I don't think I can come to too much harm because the floor is crowded with snogging couples and they are playing the 'Tennisknee Waltz' or some such tune calculated to act as an emetic if you do not have the strength to shove your fingers down your throat. All I will have to do is change my weight from one foot to the other and hope that she does not leave her plates lying about where harm can come to them. It might even be the start of something beautiful. I push her deep into the scrum of bodies so that none of the herberts standing around the side of the floor can see me making a berk of myself and wait for the loudest of the boum, boum, *boums* before gliding my left foot forward with an easy flowing motion that catches her just above the instep.

'Sorry,' I say. 'The floor's a bit fast tonight, isn't it?'

'Are you barmy?' she says. 'Surely you can do a waltz?'

'I think it's you,' I say. 'You've got me all excited. That's a lovely perfume you're wearing. What is it? I'd like to get some for my Mum.' Natalie does not look as flattered as I would like her to be and I am swift to try and set her mind at ease. 'For her birthday,' I say. 'She'd like to smell like you, I know she would. I always get her perfume – sorry, was that your leg again?'

'No, it belonged to the man behind me,' she says. 'Can't you keep in time with the rhythm? *One*, two, three. *One*, two-ouch!'

'Sorry!' I say. I stop and pull her very close to me so that I don't have to see the look of suffering on her face. 'Let's start again. Right foot forward.' I notice one of the bouncers who was near the Orchestra Bar peering at me like he recognises me, and burrow into the centre of the floor as he beckons to one of his mates.

'What was that supposed to be?' says Natalie.

'That was the Lea shuffle,' I say. 'It's very handy when you're being crowded.'

'You've ruined my shoes,' she says. 'It's the first time I've worn them, too.'

'They're lovely,' I say. 'I like that snakeskin pattern.'

'That's not snakeskin,' she says. 'That's where you've been standing all over them with your rubber soles!'

Before I can make further headway, there is a roll on the drums and Greasebonce, the MC, grabs the mike and leaps to the edge of the stage like he has plans to shove it up somebody's jacksy. 'Yes, folks. It's the moment you've all been waiting for!' he trills. 'Let's have you all on the floor. It's time for our Elimination Spot Waltz!'

I have a picture of couples circling round the floor trying to eliminate each other's spots until the duo that has accumulated the biggest pile of blackheads is declared the winner and given a giant jar of Germolene. It is not the kind of thought you want to dwell on.

'We don't want to do this, do we?' I say.

'Oh yes we do!' Natalie grips me tightly. 'The couple last week won a colour TV set.'

'They're giving them away as paperweights at the moment,' I say.

Natalie does not reply. An expression of grin-and-bear-it determination has settled on her face.

'Carry on dancing, boys and girls.' I think Natalie fancies Greasebonce. There is a repulsive glint of desire in her over-made up eyes as she gazes upon his plum-coloured, braid-trimmed jacket and the yellow ruffles piled up on his chest like the overspill from a cracked boiled egg.

I grit my teeth and concentrate hard. One, two, three-ouch! One, two, three-ouch! I am not too worried because we will soon be eliminated. I have never won anything in my life. Boum-ting! The cymbals clash and my hampton gives a nervous twitch – it always does when somebody bashes a couple of cymbals together. Greasebonce leaps from the stage and makes his way to the middle of the floor.

'Everybody behind me—' he pauses so that all the stupid birds can go, 'Oooh!' – 'off the floor please.'

'That's us, isn't it?' I say.

'No!' Natalie clings to me with an intensity that I would be happy to experience in different circumstances. 'Carry on dancing!'

Now that half the people have left the floor it is much

more difficult to hide and I begin to feel a right Charlie as the crowds build up to clock my diabolical style. Everybody else circles round us like Indians attacking a wagon train and Sid is there, rising and falling as if dancing on a switchback. Gloria has her head turned over her left shoulder as if he has bad breath – knowing Sid, he probably has.

Boum-ting! Surely, this time I will be delivered.

'The first ten gentlemen to bring me a pair of lady's tights or stockings!'

'Ooh!' Natalie whips up her skirts and starts undoing one of her stockings. She has a nice pair of legs, I must say. It is quite sexy, really, because all around me, birds are flashing their goodies. Sid is taking it very seriously because his bird is lying on her back and he is peeling her tights off in one continuous pull. 'Come on!' Natalie clearly thinks that I should be lending a hand so I start fiddling with one of her suspenders. I make a lousy job of it because I want to make blooming certain that we do not get in the first ten. Also, because I quite enjoy the feeling of her soft, silky flesh beneath my fingers and the thought that I am touching her up in front of hundreds of people. 'Oh, give it here!' She brushes my fingers away and pulls her stocking down to knee level as Greasebonce announces that he has his ten couples and that they have all been eliminated. Most of the blokes just picked their partners up and carried them over to him, so the striptease was unnecessary.

I am now getting desperate. The floor seems as wide as Horse Guards' Parade and I hear a burst of laughter as I try and do a turn and sock some bloke on the hooter with my elbow.

'You're dancing the wrong way!' hisses Natalie.

'I know I am,' I say. 'I've never been properly taught.'

'I mean, you're dancing the wrong way round the floor,' she says. 'That's why you keep bumping into people.' Amazing, isn't it? I never realised it was like the dodgems. I do another turn and kick her so hard in the shin that she is dancing an Irish jig when there comes another bash on the cymbals.

'Ooh we are having fun, aren't we?' says Greasebonce. 'What are we having?'

'Fun! !' shout the idiots lining the floor.

'That's right,' says Greasebonce. 'Now, how many couples on the floor are married?' Half a dozen hands go up. 'You're out! You've got your prize already. Carry on dancing.'

'Why are you just standing there?' says Natalie.

'Everybody is looking at me,' I say. 'I'm making a fool of myself. Let's get off.'

'Don't be stupid,' she says. 'We could win a prize. I'll lead. You follow me.'

I do not think that I have ever felt a bigger berk in my life than in the few minutes that I stumble round that floor. Natalie is trying to do the whole 'Come Dancing' bit and I am more flushed than the toilet in a prune tasters' commune. I wish the floor would open and swallow me up. Why won't the music stop? Why—? Boum-ting!

'Oh! It's exciting, isn't it! What shall we do now?' Greasebonce pretends not to hear when one of the band tells him. 'Right! Who's got a birthday in November?'

'I have,' I say.

'Ssh!' says Natalie. 'He'll have us off.'

'Me, me!' I shout. I am practically jumping up and down.

'Anybody else?' There is a long pause and then another geezer sticks his mit in the air.

'Right! We've got our finalists. Everybody else off the floor, please.'

'Oh my gawd!' I close my eyes.

'Smashing! You are clever.' When I open them again, Natalie is looking at me with something approaching admiration.

'It's nothing,' I say. 'I get involved in a lot of road accidents as well.'

To my horror, I see that Greasebonce is approaching us with a couple of balloons in his mit. 'Right!' he chortles. 'One of these on each of your heels. The first couple to burst both the other couple's balloons is the winner.'

'I can't stand it!' I whimper.

'Don't be like that,' says Natalie. 'You've been stamping on my feet all evening. Surely a couple of balloons won't give you any trouble?'

'Couldn't they just shoot me?' I say.

'Finalists at opposite ends of the ballroom, please.'

'Good luck, Natalie!' Gloria is grinning like an oval xylophone and next to her I see Sid bury his face in his hands and start shaking his head. I feel like a prisoner dragging an iron ball as I trudge down to the band rostrum. If it was near one of the exit doors I would make a break for it.

'When you're ready, maestro.' Greasebonce turns to Ted Bennett – him of 'Ted Bennett and the Bennettmen' – and Ted stops picking his nose with his baton and wipes it under his armpit – his baton, not his hooter. Everybody is cheering and shouting and I wish I could feel the adrenalin running through my blood – come to that, I wish I could feel my blood running through anything. 'Ready, steady, dance!'

'Right,' says Natalie, very firm and determined. 'Keep

cool. Left foot back. One, two, three. One, two, BANG!

I have only stood on my own balloon, haven't I? A roar of laughter goes up and something inside me snaps. A Lea can only take so much. If these herberts want to take the piss then I will give them something they can really get their teeth into. Fed up with trying to dance, I grab Natalie and charge towards the other couple who are gliding towards us like they are on roller skates. I see the bloke's eyes widen in terror but it is too late for him to take defensive action. He is locked into a complicated spin turn and at my mercy. I am not quite certain what I intend to do with the lovely creature in my arms but, as so often happens with me, fate takes the decision. I get my feet wrapped round the balloon string and pitch forward so that I throw Natalia on the floor. There are two bangs almost simultaneously and a roar from the crowd. When I prize my hooter off the boards it is to find that both the opposition balloons have been burst and that ours is still intact. The other couple are hopping mad and Greasebonce is clearly undecided what to do. Fortunately, Sid makes an opportune appearance.

'Great dancing, Timmy,' he says. 'That last stem christie was really something. You'll soon be on to parallels.'

'Dancing!' says the beaten finalist in a voice that sounds as if someone has opened an umbrella down his throat. 'He can't dance a step! He threw his partner at us.'

'That's his ballet training,' says Sid. 'You reveal your ignorance when you talk like that. The Russians have been after him for years.'

'Rubbish!' says the bloke.

'Careful, Dame Margot!' says Sid. 'If you don't learn to be a good loser my boot will be doing a double reverse spin turn up your khyber!'

'That's nice!' says the bloke. 'That's very nice.'

'I was afraid you'd think so,' says Sid. 'Tell me, are those white streaks in your hair natural or do you keep pigeons?'

'I don't know quite what to do,' says Greasebonce.

'I'd declare him the winner,' says Sid, pointing at me. 'It would be nasty if violence broke out and the hall was wrecked. I happened to be here the last time there was a spot of bother and I remember how unpleasant it was. It took months to get the place operational again – and, talking about operations, I'm trying to remember how many stitches the MC had—'

'The winners, ladies and gentlemen! Let's give them a big hand.' Greasebonce snatches up my mit like he is scared it might blow away and raises it aloft with Natalie's. There is a roar from the crowd and a louder roar from the bloke we were dancing against. Sid has just stood on his instep.

'Here, blow your nose on this,' says my brother-in-law, wrenching the silk rose from his partner's dress so that her knockers bounce out like they have been rung up on a till.

'Ooh, how wonderful!' squeals Natalie. She clings to my arm and only breaks away long enough to hug Gloria. Sid catches my eye and winks. 'Nice going, Timmo,' he says. 'We'll be in like Flynn after this lot.'

'But when are we going to talk to them about getting on a boat?' I say.

'There's plenty of time for that,' says Sid. 'The night is young. Go and collect your prize.'

Natalie is thrilled out of her teeny mind because she cops a wicker basket full of picnic stuff and I am not exactly choked to receive a blooming great bottle of champagne. We even get our photograph taken by a bloke from the

Sentinel. It is practically film-star treatment by SW12 standards.

'Ooh, I can't wait to get it home and look at it properly,' coos Natalie, hugging her basket. 'The knives have got bone handles.'

'Fabulous,' breathes Sid. 'We'll be able to christen the beakers with Timmy's champagne.'

'Oh yeah,' says Natalie, looking at Gloria.

'Yes,' says Gloria. They look at each other like their minds are keeping pace with Sid's and I have the feeling that we may be on the verge of a nooky feast. Certainly both birds seem to be much more attuned to my magnetism since I revealed my terpsichorean talent (it's all right, you can't get arrested for it.)

'Is it all right if we go to your place?' says Gloria.

'Yes,' says Natalie. 'I've got enough Nescafé.'

'Nescafé?' says Sid. 'You just give us the goblets.'

'I beg your pardon!' says Natalie, coming on like Mary Whitehouse finding that someone has dropped the bog paper down the Karsi.

'I said, give us the goblets,' says Sid. 'Honestly, girls, you do jump to conclusions.'

'You live alone, do you?' I say as I snuggle down with Natalie in the back of Sid's Rover.

'I do when my husband is away,' says the lovely creature.

'Is he at sea, as well?' I ask.

'Completely,' she says.

'You must get very lonely,' I say, giving her arm a squeeze and nuzzling her barnet – it is like a pan scourer with all that lacquer on it.

'I do,' she says. 'Especially at nights. It's not sex.'

'No, of course not,' I say hurriedly – I mean, I would never think of that, would I?

'It's the companionship. Somebody to talk over the events of the day with.'

'Exactly,' I say. 'I know just how you feel.'

This is not strictly true but I am working on it. I run my hand up Natalie's arm, lightly dust my digits over her bristols – almost accidentally, like I did not know they were there – and then descend for a warm, friendly squeeze of the hand. She smiles up at me and I kiss her on the end of the nose. Tender stuff, I am certain you will agree and not far removed from the love interest in a Walt Disney movie. Still, there are more ways of skinning a cat than by leaving a dead mouse at the bottom of your spin drier, and a lot of storms start with a small ripple running across the surface of still water – watch the old movies on the telly if you don't believe me.

'You're different to what I thought you were,' says Natalie. 'Underneath, you're shy, aren't you?'

It is always favourite to agree with this kind of statement because it allows the bird to plot her own downfall. They all have this fantasy about introducing a shy, inexperienced boy to the delights of sex – even if they have never found them themselves – and you can discover yourself immersed in a lot of grumble and grunt if you let them have their way.

'I wouldn't say that,' I say awkwardly.

'Wouldn't say what?' says Sid getting into the car and reaching across to open the door for Gloria – I don't know what he was doing to her in the doorway but it looked as if he was trying to sit her on the doorknob.

'He's trying to tell me he knows what it's all about,' says Natalie.

'Don't believe him,' says Sid. 'He's a babe in arms where you-know-what is concerned. Keeps asking me embarrassing questions about where babies come from. He tries to talk big but it's all a front.'

'I thought so!' Natalie sounds pleased with herself and grabs hold of my arm. 'There, there, Timmy. Don't be frightened. Aunty Natalie isn't going to eat you.'

'If you'd have told me that earlier, I wouldn't have come,' I say.

'All talk,' says Sid. 'Coarse but harmless.' He winks at me and shoves the car into gear.

117 Marsh View Gardens is not a lot different to 119 and not totally dissimilar to 115. I don't take a lot of notice because it is late when we get there and there is more activity from the neighbouring houses. An old biddy pops out of 115 and says that some men have been looking for Natalie and the curtains of 119 are stirring as if fanned by a strong breeze.

'Nosy old bitch,' says Natalie, though I don't know who she is talking about.

'They're terrible round me, as well,' says Gloria. 'The tongues never stop.'

'What a lovely thought,' says Sid rubbing his hands together.

'You are awful, Sid!' says Gloria delivering a playful push. 'I'm not surprised your first wife left you.'

'What's that?' I say.

Sid looks uncomfortable. 'Gladys,' he says. 'You remember Gladys?' There is a note of pleading in his voice

'Oh yes,' I say. 'I didn't think you could bear to mention her.'

'I can't usually,' says Sid. 'But you know what it's like. Sometimes the past opens up like a book.'

'I'll get the glasses,' says Natalie. It is clear that Sid's words have touched her.

'That's right,' says Gloria. 'Don't let's get morbid.'

'It's a lovely picnic basket,' says Sid. 'You did well there, Timmo. How are you doing with that bottle?'

I don't have to answer him because the cork shatters the Toby Jug on the mantelpiece and the champagne soaks the china ducks like they have flown into a heavy rain storm.

'You're a suave bugger, aren't you?' says Sid. 'Noel Coward must have snuffed it without a care in the world when he knew you were following on behind.'

'It doesn't matter,' says Natalie. 'I never liked that jug anyway.'

'I'm sorry,' I say. 'I—'

'Don't worry about it!' Natalie ruffles my hair and pushes me into an armchair. 'I'm in too good a mood to worry about that.' She takes the bottle from my hand and starts filling the glasses. Sid gives me the thumbs-up sign behind her back.

'Shall I put a record on?' says Gloria.

'That old cow next door will start thumping on the wall,' says Natalie. 'Still, I don't care. It's Saturday night, isn't it?'

'That's right,' says Sid. 'Let yourself go. Let it all hang out.' He unbuttons his shirt down to the beginnings of his paunch and runs his hand up the back of Gloria's leg underneath her skirt.

'Stop it! You'll give him ideas.'

'Natalie knows how to handle him,' says Sid. 'Come here!' He hauls Gloria on to his lap and starts double parking his lips.

'Don't you want a drink?' says Natalie. Sid continues trying to rearrange Gloria's cakehole, so she comes over to me and perches on the edge of the armchair. 'You'd like a bit, wouldn't you?'

'Definitely,' I say. I take the glass and stare at her

knockers over the top of it. She must have loosened something while I wasn't looking. She is wearing a black bra and I can just see the lacy bit at the edge.

'What are you looking at?' she says.

'Nothing,' I say.

'Nothing! That's not very nice.' Natalie looks down at her bristols with a hurt expression on her face.

'On the contrary,' I say. 'That's *very* nice.'

'Oh,' she says, her voice perking up. 'You're a bit forward, aren't you?'

'Some of me is,' I say glancing down to where Percy is beginning to play Snakes and Ladders up the inside of my y-fronts. From the feel of him, he has just thrown a double.

'Cheeky boy.' Natalie takes a sip of her champagne and ruffles the hair at the back of my neck. I turn my head and kiss the inside of her arm. 'It's nice, isn't it?'

She is talking about the champagne and I nod. 'We earned it, didn't we? I'm sorry I dumped you on your fife. It's all right, is it?' I don't wait for an answer but pull Natalie closer to me and start massaging her sit feature. Sid and Gloria have now disappeared behind the settee and I don't think they are looking for a missing caster.

'It's getting better,' says Natalie. She tilts back my chin with her forefinger and settles on my north and south like she is frightened that she might bruise my lips. Very gentle, it is. I squeeze her tighter and pull her on to my lap, parking my champagne glass beside the armchair. From now on I am going to need two hands. Natalie dips her fingers in her glass and pushes them inside my shirt so that they lie cold and damp against my chest. I shiver because I know that I am expected to and feed a couple of inches of brewer's bung into her cakehole. This has all the makings of a cosy evening before they discovered television and I begin to feel more kindly disposed towards Sid and his quest for nautical information. They way things are going I am going to get my two pounds thirty pence back with interest. Natalie prises her lips off mine long enough to take a swig of champagne and then thoughtfully pours the rest of the glass over my trousers.

'Oh dear,' I say. 'I'll have to take them off, won't I?'

'You can hang them on top of his,' says Natalie. 'My dress is a bit damp, too.'

Sid's clobber is building up on the back of the settee like the vicar's wife's counter at a jumble sale and I strip down to my Y-fronts before you can say Roger Carpenter.

'You're losing your inhibitions, I see,' says Natalie, stepping out of her dress and looking round for somewhere to put it – there is hardly a spare surface left.

'I was thinking of keeping them on,' I say. OK it's a daft mumble but it gives her a natural opening to put her wicked fingers to work in the ferret fondling department.

'No chance,' she husks, pushing me back against the settee and pursing her lips. 'Let's see what you're made of.'

'Sugar and spice, and all things nice,' I say.

'That's little girls,' she says. 'You're a puppy dog's tail.' She leans forward to chew my lower lip and the tips of her boobs brush my chest. It is a very sexy feeling and that is what I am soon getting at crutch level as Natalie's banana peelers get to work.

'That's not a puppy dog's tail,' she says.

'I just traded it in for a pink mamba,' I tell her. I slip my hand into her panties and she tightens her grip on my prod rod as I set my pinkies typing 'Now is the time for all good men to come' on the inside of her jive hive. A few more hits or misses and it is clear that we are both ready for the main feature. What she is doing to my underpants clearly threatens the tensility of the material and with clothes the price they are these days, no man can afford to destitute himself in the cause of love. I prise my sit feature off the settee long enough to whip my Y-fronts down to my knees and allow Natalie to conduct them on the rest of their journey to the floor. I am now lying naked on the settee with a hard like the Eddystone lighthouse flashing a warning to low flying aircraft and Natalie is straining forward as she reaches behind her for her bra strap: It is a pretty sight – well, she is – and only capped by that magic moment when she skips out of her knicks and attempts to snuff out my doughnut duffer. One knee on either side of my thighs and she grabs my hard handful and tickles her fuzz with its glowing tip.

'What a lot I slot,' she breathes, easing herself down with a sigh.

'All right, are you?' Trust Sid to have a horn in – not literally, thank goodness – at such a moment of private ecstasy. I have been sparing sensitive readers a description of the noises wafting up from behind the settee but it is as clear as the sweat pouring off Sid's boat race that sexual intercourse of a very energetic kind has just come to an end.

'Piss off, Sid!' I say. 'Go and read the TV Times.'

'Fancy a drink?' says Sid. 'There's a lot of this champagne left.' He takes a swig from the bottle and pours some over my belly. I jump about six inches into the air and Natalie cops the benefit.

'Ooh! That's cold.'

'Stop messing about, Sid!'

'I can't help it. I always feel chirpy after a bit of the other. Where's that record player?'

'Don't worry about me, will you?' says Gloria, rising up from behind the sofa and picking some carpet fluff off her generous knockers – 'Oh no! You're lying on my dress! Do you mind!' She leans across the back of the settee to get at her dress and I can't resist giving one of her pink Manchesters a nibble.

'Dirty sod!' says Natalie.

'Let's get on the floor,' I say. 'The springs are cutting into my bum.' I give Gloria's grumble a tickle and by the time that Sid has put on the *Confessions* LP – available from all high-class record shops, folks – I have sunk to the carpet with both our new friends. This time, I am on top and I drive into Natalie like she is the last berth on a crowded car ferry. Gloria is doing something very naughty to me from behind and Sid turns up the volume on the record player and takes another hefty swig from the champagne bottle.

'Ride 'er cowboy!' he shouts. 'Up the blues!'

'Do give over!' says Gloria. 'You'll wake all the neighbours.'

At that very instant, there is a loud thumping on the wall and Natalie groans. 'That's Mrs Burgess,' she says.

'Shut up, you old bag!' Sid puts his mouth against the wall beside the fireplace and shouts at the top of his voice.

It is clear that he is pissed out of his mind. It is so inconsiderate. How can I be expected to perform in these circumstances? I grit my teeth and try and work up a measured rhythm. Thump! Thump! Thump! I am not certain whether it is me, Sid or Mrs Burgess. Everybody is dishing it out.

'Come here!' Sid pulls Gloria to her feet and starts having it off with her against the wall that separates us from Mrs Burgess's front room. The noise is diabolical and a couple of bits of plaster fall down. The light is swinging backwards and forwards like a pendulum.

'OOOH!' Natalie has closed her eyes and her mouth is opening wider with every O. I am glad that she is coming because I have the feeling that the evening cannot go on like this much longer. I am all for a party atmosphere but this is getting ridiculous. Judging my moment like a surfer picking a wave I hug Natalie to me and roar in on the crest of a breaker.

'AAAARGh!' The white tip curls and I wipe out in a froth of honeyed warmth. Sid, too, is steaming up one of the china ducks with his knackered breath and I sense that he has just enjoyed a similar pleasure to myself.

'That was lovely,' says Natalie, giving me a squeeze. 'Be a doll and turn the record player down.'

I stagger to my feet and kick over the champagne bottle. It does not matter because it is now empty.

'Don't turn it off,' says Sid. 'I like a bit of music.' He starts dancing round, stark bollock naked. 'Oh, a life on the ocean wave, a life on the ocean wave—!!'

I look across to the window and see that there is a gap where the curtains have not been drawn properly. 'Weigh, hey, up she rises! Weigh, hey, up she rises. How do you fancy a hornpipe, darling?' Sid starts giggling and climbs on to the settee.

I have never seen him so Chopin. The banging from next door starts again and Sid leans forward to turn up the record player. He pitches forward and knocks a pile of records on the floor. I help him up on my way to the window and glance out before pulling the curtains closed. What I see makes my blood run colder than a penguin's chuff. Two blokes are coming up the garden path carrying suitcases.

'Sid!' I scream, diving for my pants. 'There's someone coming.'

Sid starts to bounce up and down on the settee like a chimp on a trampoline. 'It's not me,' he says. 'I couldn't. I'm knackered. Rule Britannia! Britannia rules the waves. Britains never, never will be – good evening.'

The two men framed in the doorway do not answer Sid. They are breathing heavily and certainly, when I glimpsed them, they were hurrying towards the front door. You can almost hear their eyeballs clicking as they take in the scene. I manage to get my second leg into my Y-fronts and pull them up round my waist. The girls snatch at whatever lies handy and hold it in front of them.

'Welcome ashore, maties,' says Sid. 'You have a good trip, did you? I'm glad you've shown up because there are a few things my friend wants to ask you. I've got to—'

'You bastard!'

'No need to get excited,' squeaks Sid. 'We were only playing charades – ooh!' He stops talking when one of the herberts belts him in the Newingtons. The girls start screaming, Mrs Burgess is still trying to bash the wall down and the record player packs it in with a shriek of agony second only to that of the geezer who cops both Sid's plates in his mug as our hero swings from the light fitting and lashes out with his tootsies. It is very Errol Flynn, with the subtle difference that the light fitting stayed in the ceiling when Errol swung from it. This one comes down with a blinding flash and a cloud of plaster. The room is plunged into darkness and all that can be heard are screams and thuds as Sid and I try to avoid copping an Irish face-lift.

In fact, we do rather better than that and by the time the police car arrives (Mrs Burgess must have rung for it) both the homecoming mariners are stretched out on the floor taking forty blinks and Natalie is having hysterics.

'Oh, Henry! Henry!' she screams. 'Why did you have to hit him with the coal scuttle?'

'Because he was trying to rearrange my cluster with a poker!' shouts Sid. 'Control yourself, woman! A few stitches can only improve that Jem Mace. Get out there and stall those bules.'

At the same instant there is a banging on the side door and both Sid and I put a foot in the same trouser leg.

'We've got to get out of here!' says Sid unnecessarily. 'Grab your clobber and follow me.'

'Supposing there's someone waiting at the back?' I say.

'There won't be,' says Sid. 'Ta ta, Gloria. Thanks for everything.'

Gloria is cradling the nut of one of the blokes who is groaning on the ground. 'You bastard!' she says. 'What am I going to tell him?'

'Tell him you love him,' says Sid.

CHAPTER TWO

In which Timmy and Sid travel to Southampton and serve upper class Caroline Rankin and her mummy and daddy, passengers on SS *Tern*.

Sid is right. There is no one waiting outside the back door. We are over the wall, through the cucumber frame and two streets away before I realise that I have taken the wrong jacket.

'That's marvellous,' I say. 'They'll get me for thieving now. What a wonderful end to an evening. We must do this more often.'

'You're not nice when you're sarcastic,' says Sid. 'What's it got in it, anything worth nicking?'

'They're going to trace us from the car,' I bleat. 'Oh my gawd. Why didn't I stop at home and watch World in Agony? I can't stand doing any more bird.'

'Fifty quid!' says Sid, thumbing through a bundle of notes he has produced from one of the pockets of the jacket. 'Blimey, he must have been planning to buy Britain.'

'We'll have to send it back,' I say, getting desperate. 'I don't want to get lumbered with that.'

'Uum,' says Sid. 'We'll have to see.' He puts the money in his back pocket and produces another piece of paper. 'This is interesting. "Memo to cabin staff. Owing to the breakdown of the refrigeration system, the ship will call at Southampton for repairs. Crew members who obtain passes from me will be allowed ashore until 0600 hours on the 24th. P. Pervis, Purser. SS *Tern*".'

'Lucky swines,' I say. 'That's where we ought to be.'

'Just what I was thinking,' says Sid thoughtfully. 'It's Waterloo for Southampton, isn't it?'

'What are you on about?' I say. 'You're not thinking of taking their places, are you?'

'This seems like as good a time as any to take our leave of the old country,' says Sid. 'I can always send Rosie a postcard from Port Said.'

'But what about when the other blokes roll up?' I say. 'The police aren't going to hold them, are they?'

'I don't know so much,' says Sid. 'One of their suitcases burst open during our little frackarse and I couldn't help clocking a butcher's at the contents.'

'Three month's dirty washing?' I say.

'Not so much as a soiled cuff let alone an unmentionable stain,' says Sid. 'Watches.' He dives a hand into his pocket and produces a flash job with a metal bracelet and enough dials to launch a space probe. 'Handsome, isn't it? There were about two hundred like that.'

'And you nicked one, Sid? That's downright dishonest. You don't have any scruples, do you?'

'I got one for you as well,' says Sid.

'Oh.' It's difficult to know what to say, isn't it? I don't want to hurt Sid's feelings even though he has been naughty. A generous impulse should not be punished, especially when in Sid's case it may never be repeated. I shove the watch deep into my pocket and clear my throat. 'Ta, Sid. You think they were – er half inched, do you?'

'Or smuggled,' says Sid. 'They were clearly Bernard Dillons, those blokes. The way he went about my person with that poker was strictly non-Marquess of Queensbury.'

'But we can't just take their places, Sid.'

'Why not? If my surmise is correct, Purser Pervis is going to be two men short tomorrow morning and he'd rather have us than nothing. It's much more free and easy in the Merchant Marine, Timmo.'

I am not certain that Sid is right – in fact I am never certain that Sid is right – but I nip home, pack my Chelsea hold-all – Second Division! Diabolical, isn't it? and leave a note for Mum and Dad. It is a bit like running away from home which I have not done since I was nine and did not have the bus fare to get to Clapham Junction. When I got home nobody had realised that I had gone.

I get the tube from Clapham South to Waterloo station and find Sid putting the boot in a drinks dispenser. 'Bleeding thing has run out of cups,' he says.

'I wondered why the front of your trousers was steaming,' I say.

'It's embarrassing, isn't it?' says Sid. 'This bleeding country is going to the dogs. Nobody cares any more.' He gives the dispenser another savage kick and a stream of coins pours out of one of the slots. They don't have to pour far because Sid's hands are under the opening as if drawn by powerful magnets. 'A little something towards the dry cleaning bill,' he says.

'What's the train situation?' I say, looking round nervously and half hoping that there isn't one.

'The twelve twenty,' says Sid. 'Better get the tickets, I suppose.' He removes a roll of notes from his back pocket and winks at me as he reads my worried expression. 'I don't expect they came by them gainfully, Timmo. We're doing society a favour by putting them back in circulation.' He shoves a couple of coins into my hand. 'Go and buy us some bars of chocolate.'

He wanders off towards the booking hall and I look at the coins. One is Irish and one has a picture of Martin Peters on it. One thing about us leaving the country:

Britain can only be a more prosperous place with Sid out of it.

Sid has bought the tickets – he tried to get a reduction for night travel but the bloke would not wear it – and we are walking towards the barrier when there is the sound of agitated movement behind us.

'For heaven's sake, Martha! Move yourself!'

'Don't raise your voice to me, John Rankin. It wasn't me who looked up the trains.'

'Why are there no blasted porters? Skulking red swine!'

'Oh, Daddy, please!'

Bearing down on us in a welter of pigskin cases are a tweedy duo of advanced middle age and a bird of quite exceptional fanciability. They are all staggering under the weight of several suitcases and one gets the impression that this is something they are not used to doing. Ever chivalrous and eager to get on good terms with a nice bit of crumpet, I step forward with a willing smile on my boat race.

'Can I give you a hand?' I say.

My remark is addressed to the bint but it is Mr Rankin who answers. 'Yes,' he snaps. 'There's a cabin trunk by the taxi.' He turns his back on me and starts to argue with the geezer on the barrier who says he won't let him past without a ticket. 'Damn it, man!' I hear him shouting. 'My father was on the board of the London and North Eastern when it was making a profit!'

'That would be awfully sweet of you,' purrs Mrs Rankin. 'We've had the most awful struggle to find a taxi.'

'And the man was absolutely beastly because Daddy didn't have any change to tip him with,' says Miss Rankin raping me with her mince pies. She is wearing a fluffy little white hat with a pom pom in the middle of it. On anybody else it would look bloody stupid.

'What a bloody stupid hat,' says Sid as we stagger along under the weight of what looks like a two ton loaf of Hovis. 'I wish you'd learn to keep your blooming mouth shut.'

'Have you seen what it says on this trunk?' I say. 'They're sailing on the *Tern*, too.'

As soon I read the words I see a picture of Miss Rankin leaning over the ship's rail and gazing towards the setting sun. She is alone and a faint zephyr stirs her lustrous barnet. Moving towards her with the languid grace of a young puma is myself. She senses that I am approaching and turns with a radiant smile on her face. 'Timothy!' Her arms reach out and – BANG! Some dozy syrup has nearly cut me in half with his electrical chuffer.

'You oughtn't to be out at night, mate. Nobody can see you!'

Sid's words spark off an ugly spate of agrochat which I will not repeat for fear of disturbing those sensitive about matters of race and colour. Suffice to say that it takes up so much time that we get on to the platform just as the guard is shaping up to blow his whistle.

'My God, I thought you'd made off with it!' says Mr Rankin demonstrating once more that he is not overburdened with charm. 'How the devil did it get that dent in it?'

'The cabby must have done it,' says Sid. 'He said you were the meanest git he had ever come across.'

'I'm so sorry I can't give you something for a cup of tea,' gushes Mrs Rankin.

'Not even a lump of suger?' says Sid.

'Thanks most awfully,' says Miss Rankin. 'It was absolutely super of you.'

The look on her Jem Mace makes up for everything and I am still thinking about it as we settle back in our second class compartment and the train pulls out of the station.

'You've got that stupid expression on your mug, again,'

says Sid. 'You don't want to entertain any hopes there. She wouldn't use you to scrape a Richard the Third off the back of her shoe.'

'Who?' I say, trying to look innocent.

'That bird,' says Sid. 'Miss Poshknickers. You've got the hots for her, haven't you? Why do you always go for the same type? If you broadened your horizons a bit you could get rejected by a far wider selection of judies.'

I don't answer him but gaze out of the window until I drift into a dream in which Natalie's old man is chasing me up the metal rungs on the side of an enormous funnel. When I get to the top he lunges at me and I topple backwards, falling, falling into the smoke. It seems that I am never going to reach the bottom and then – woomp! I land in something soft and suffocating.

I open my eyes and find that I have slipped sideways so that my head has dropped into Sid's lap. 'Get out!' he screams. 'Supposing someone looked through the window? You've even dribbled over my zipper. It's disgusting!'

'Don't get your knickers in a twist, Sid,' I say. 'We're here, that's the main thing.'

The inside of my mouth tastes like a vulture's shaving mug and I would give ten quid of Sid's money to be back in my cosy little pit at Scraggs Lane.

'Ah, there you are. I thought you'd skulked off. Get the trunk out to a taxi, will you?' Rankin looms up out of the damp mist and I place a restraining arm on Sid's sleeve.

'Control yourself, Sid,' I say. 'We could get a good tip out of this in the long run. He's on the boat, remember.'

'At the moment he is,' mutters Sid. 'If he keeps on like that he could find himself getting his feet wet on the walk home!'

Miss Rankin sets out to charm me with a smile and succeeds beyond her wildest dreams. 'It's *so* kind of you to help us,' she says.

'It's nothing,' I say. 'I expect I'll be seeing a lot more of you later.' It is unfortunate, perhaps, that the delivery of this remark coincides with the bird hooking her skirt on a trolley and revealing an attractively shaped scotch up to the thigh pit. 'I-er mean that I could be serving on the good ship *Tern* and that we'll probably be coming on top of each other – I mean, across each other.' Why do I always have to become something less than my cool sophisticated self when I meet a bird I fancy? 'Allow me.' I drop my end of the trunk so that it smashes against Sid's ankles, and step forward briskly to free the skirt.

'What the devil do you think you're doing?' snaps Mr Rankin.

'Just keeping his hand in,' groans Sid.

'Caroline!' Something about Mrs Rankin's voice must put the mockers up me because I wrench savagely at the skirt and in so doing dislodge the brake on the trolley. There is a loud ripping noise and the trolley lurches forward taking Caroline's skirt with it. It bashes against the trunk which quivers for a moment and then topples on to the line.

'You stupid idiot!'

I have just managed to stop the trolley when we hear the express coming. VROOOOM!!!

'Do something!' screams Mrs Rankin.

I grab Caroline and take a step backwards. BANG! There is a noise like someone dropping a flat iron into a crate of eggs and the air fills with confetti – only it is not confetti. It is the remains of the Rankins' wardrobe. I remove a rubberised corset that has become draped across my face and hand it to Mr Rankin.

'I think this must be yours, sir', I say.

CHAPTER THREE

In which Timmy and Sid find their way aboard the *Tern* and Timmy is placated by Muna, a shapely stowaway prepared to sink to any length to avoid her presence being revealed.

'Very shrewd, that was,' says Sid. 'Telling him we were going to be on the boat. He's going to go straight to the captain, isn't he?'

'We're not on the boat yet, Sid,' I say.

'We start off with a black mark against us all because of your insatiable craving for upper class crumpet. Right, here we are. Adapt a nautical roll to your gait and take your lead from me.'

We are walking along a quayside past a row of dirty great boats pulled up like cabs on a rank. Most of them are pretty quiet but the SS *Tern* is a blaze of lights and has a cluster of bodies on her two gangways. Sid approaches the gangway towards the stern and beckons to me to follow. With a few yards to go, he produces his driving licence and waves it under the hooter of the bloke on guard.

'CID,' he says. 'We'd like a few words with Henry Smallwood and his mate.'

'Arthur Drooley?' says the man, brightening up. 'You'll have to get a move on. We're weighing anchor in twenty minutes.'

'That'll be enough,' I say. 'Where do we find him?'

'Deck C, cabin 148,' says the bloke. 'It's Parkis, isn't it?'

Sid rubs his hands together and nods. 'Yeh. Still, it's better than rain.'

He pressed on leaving the bloke bewildered. 'He was talking about Pakistanis, not it being parky!' I say.

'Was he?' says Sid. 'Oh well, it doesn't matter. We're on board that's the main thing. We'll lie low until we're out of the Channel and it's too late to turn back. Then we'll report to the Purser. He should welcome us with open arms.'

Sid can be very optimistic sometimes, but I am not so confident as we make our way along a dimly lit companion-way and try to read the signs leading to the other decks. 'Doesn't even mention Deck C,' I say.

'I don't expect the passengers ever go there,' says Sid. 'The next floor down will be water, mark my words.'

'Pssst!' says a voice from the shadows.

'Just a little,' says Sid. 'What's it got to do with you?'

'I'm looking for a steward,' says an upper crust female voice. 'My tap's dripping and it's driving me mad.'

'Look no further, madam,' says Sid. 'I will address myself to your problem forthwith.' Sid's eagerness is understandable.

The bird's hair tumbles enticingly round her shoulders and her knockers look like autumn in the melon fields. What I can see of them is considerable because the neckline of her silk nightdress makes a V as if it is trying to stab her in the belly button.

'I was beginning to get desperate,' says the woman, stepping to one side so that Sid can brush past her. 'Have you got everything you need?'

'Do you want me to give you a hand, Sid?' I say.

Sid thrusts his bag against my chest. 'I'll see you in the cabin,' he says. 'Don't sit up.'

Before I can say anything else, the door has been closed in my face. How very typical. My brother-in-law is obviously in robust condition. He had it off with Gloria a couple of times to my certain knowledge and is now embarking on number three after a night of tedious travel and intense physical endeavour. Well done Noggett! Britain salutes you. If only the same kind of relentless endeavour could find its way to the production line. Me? I am knackered. I can't wait to see the inside of Cabin 148 and get my head down. I hope the bleeding thing is not locked.

With every flight of steps I go down the atmosphere gets more like the inside of Rudolf Nureyev's mink jockstrap and I wonder what it is going to be like when we put to sea. If we end up somewhere hot it must be unbearable unless you are a steamed pudding.

'All right then, so it's the last time you borrow my lipstick!'

'You know where you can stuff it!'

'Dirty bitch!'

At first, I think it is a couple of birds having a go at each other. Then I see that, despite the make-up, the creature flouncing out of the cabin is a bloke. 'Hello, Heavenly.' he says, changing through one hundred and eighty degrees as he sees me. 'You're a stranger round here, aren't you?'

'That's right,' I say. 'And I'm likely to stay that way.'

I may sound unkind but I always think it best to let gingers know exactly where you stand – which in my case is with my back to the bulkhead and my Elephant and Castle tighter than the knot in a piece of cotton.

The Brighton (Brighton Pier: Queer. Ed) does not warm to my words and disappears down the corridor like a balloon with a fast leak. Ah well, you can't please everybody. I approach 148 and take a deep breath. If it is locked I am going to be choked. I turn the handle and press. It is locked. Before the first two consonants of a well known four letter word beginning with SH can pass my lips, the Rory is whipped open and my jam tart takes a swift trip down to my daisies. I had been half expecting that Messrs Smallwood and Drooley would make a second appearance in my life and I automatically swing up my Oliver Twists and prepare to defend myself.

'Henry-oh!'

The voice does not belong to me but to what used to be described as a 'dusky damsel' in the exciting schoolboy romances of my youth. She has a beauty spot in the middle of her forehead and a couple of very beautiful spots on either side of her 'all the best'. You could drown in her eyes if you were the clumsy type. It is obvious that she comes from distant climes and is even more surprised to see me than vice-versa. Never slow to assert my brute mastery over a wilting frail, I press forward sideways so that I do not lock my enormous shoulders in the narrow doorway.

'What are you doing here?' I say accusingly before she can say the same thing.

'Do not send me back!' she begs. 'I will do anything.' This is good news and my action man kit promptly radios its position to the rest of my body. For sheer, downright, knockout good looks this bird is probably as classic an article as has ever strayed in front of my mince pies. I remember what the guy on the gangway said and play a hunch – I would rather play a haunch with this chick but there is no point in rushing things.

'You're from Pakistan, aren't you?' I say.

'Yes,' she gulps. 'You won't make me go back, will you? Henry said he would take me with him.'

'Well he didn't, did he?' I say, so mean that I almost frighten myself. 'He left you here?'

'That is right,' she says. 'He left me here while he went ashore. He had business to do.'

I begin to feel that the plot is getting over-complicated. 'Why didn't he take you ashore?' I ask.

'I do not want to go ashore,' she says. 'I stay here until we sail.'

'Let's get this straight,' I say. 'You were smuggled into this country?'

'That is right,' says the girl.

'But you don't want to go ashore?'

'Not now,' says the Paki smasher with a shudder. 'I am trying to escape.'

'Escape from England?' I say.

She closes her eyes and nods. 'I cannot stand any more. The weather, the digging up of the cricket pitches, the curryburgers. It is horrible!'

'I see what you mean,' I say. I mean, it does sound nasty, doesn't it? Especially the curryburgers. 'So you won't be sari to leave?' I say, injecting a note of merriment into our conversation.

The jewel of the mystic East shakes her nut from side to side. 'No,' she says. She clearly does not coco my robust wit but you can't have everything. 'Where is my Henry?'

There is a rattling sound in my left earhole which I hope is the anchor going up. 'I don't think he'll be joining us,' I say. 'I'm taking his place.'

'But he promised he would be back.'

'He ran into a spot of bother,' I say. 'Don't worry. It's nothing serious. Nothing that a few months in the chokey won't sort out.' I let my mince pies wander over the delectable bint before me and new life flows into my being – or, putting it another way, I start to get a hard on. There is fear in the bird's eyes and that always bodes well for the rigidity of my pramrod.

'What are you going to do with me?' she says.

'It's difficult,' I say, trying to look as if I am grappling with a load of agonising decision-making. 'I should hand you over.'

'No!' she begs. 'I would not take up much room. I can sleep on floor.'

'No need to go to those lengths,' I say hurriedly – if the lady wants to go to a length, I have one that is much nearer than the floor and getting further away from it with every second. 'It's my friend I'm worried about. He's expecting to share this cabin.'

'I will serve you both,' pants the lovely creature, her bristols heaving. 'You may do what you wish with me but do not send me back to Bognor Regis.'

Cabin staff laid on, I think to myself. Can't be Hyderabad to come back to your own stewardess after a hard day ministering to others. Sid can hardly reject the idea. Mind you, space is going to be at a premium. This cabin is so small that you would have to ask a cat to touch its toes before you tried to swing it.

'What's your name?' I say.

'Muna.'

'Timmy,' I say. 'My mate is called Sid. I'm afraid that he may make unspeakable demands upon you. Do you think you will be able to cope?'

'What is cope?' she says. 'Is it like blow job? I am very good at those.'

'Really?' I say, swallowing hard – which is an appropriate thing to do in the circumstances. 'How very interesting. I think I had better get my head down. I'm a bit knackered.'

'If you like, I get my head down,' says Muna, helpfully. 'Lie on the bunk. I undress you.' I am about to point out that the lady has mistaken my drift and then I think better of it. She is clearly eager to get on the right side of me and I have no doubts as to what that is at the moment.

'Er – all right,' I say. 'I am a bit – yes.' I lie down on the lower bunk and examine a knot hole above my nut. There is not a lot of room for the kiss of life or other naughty pleasures.

'Relax. You are stiff.' Well, she is partly right. If there is a wrinkle on my Marquis of Lorne it must be old age. She smiles at me with her warm, brown eyes and strokes her hand over my crutch. Percy might go off like a rat trap if she is not careful. 'You won't give me away, will you?'

'I'll think about it,' I say.

Actually, my mind is currently full of other thoughts. What my old school master used to refer to as the 'unclean' variety – 57 different kinds of them. Muna scratches her fingernail down my zipper and shivers run the length of my nunga – if they walked they would get the soles of their feet burnt. She takes the delicate metal tab between finger and thumb and pulls. For some people it is the opening bars of Beethoven's Fifth Symphony but my favourite music is made by the tiny crutch level xylophone that comes with every pair of round the houses. Played in the lower register it frequently brings tears to my thighs.

'He wants to come out,' says my new friend. 'Let us give him a taste of freedom.'

'Er-why not?' I say. I find that sparkling conversation seldom flows from my lips at these moments. I am so busy keeping an eye on what is happening that I get a crick in the neck that puts the mockers on speech. Muna slides her mit into the velvet void and I give a quick wriggle so that my pants and jeans slide down to my thighs. Muna rests her head on them so that the cleft of my heft is nodding before her mince pies and runs her tongue round the inside of her lips as if lubricating them. It may be my imagination but I think that I grow another half an inch on the spot. Muna is in no hurry to boost her protein intake but slips her hand on to my Ned Kelly and starts tightening up the curls in my nether barnet. She licks her lips again and slowly extends her tongue in time with the closing of her eyes. Just as I think she is going to make contact, her head falls back and she lightly strokes the base of my shaft. Percy could now make a dent in the side of a Centurion tank and the suspense must be playing havoc with my nervous system.

'Go on!' I breathe.

'You will let me stay here?'

'Of course,' I gasp.

'You promise?'

'Promise!'

The bird is now huffing on the end of my knob like she is trying to melt it. I had heard that these Eastern tarts were magic when it came to the sack, and this little darling seems no expection to the tool. She gives me another smouldering look and slowly parts her lips. Her hand pulls down Percy like she is drawing a pint of mild and – ooooh! I will never be able to look at a dollop of black currant ice cream again. I wonder if she does snake charming in her spare time? With that technique she could make a punctured inner tube perform the Dance of the Sugar Plum Fairy. I lie back and enjoy the delicious waves of pleasure going through me like the fruity bits through a gob stopper – and talking about fruity bits – and for that matter, talking about gob stoppers! This nice Eastern lady makes a suction cleaner seem like your old grandmother trying to suck up cold Ovaltine through a straw. I reckon they must call her 'The Mouth of the Ganges' back home.

'Ooh!' I gasp. 'No! You mustn't – ooh-er!' There is a lot more like that, only less sophisticated, and it is all I can do to keep myself to myself. 'Hang on a minute,' I say. 'Or rather, don't hang on a minute. Let's have a gander at what you've got under that sari.' Honestly, if you want to unwind, this is the way to do it. She leaves my hampton looking like a stick of Blackpool rock by the time you have licked it down to 'LACKPOO' and starts doing a graceful turn while she sheds her sari – mind you, she does a pretty graceful turn without shedding her sari as I have already discovered. It would have been nice to have enjoyed a swallow wallow but after the good time she has given me it seems only fair to introduce Percy to her banger hangar and celebrate the occasion with a spot of movement – sensitivity is my middle name. Her knockers are of the long graceful variety and I do not reckon that they have ever known the restraining influence of a bra. I stretch out my hands for them but she sways away and continues turning. Soon I will cop a butcher's at her exotic Eastern underwear. A couple of banyan leaves sewn together, no doubt, or a gossamer-thin loin cloth. In fact, she turns out to be wearing a pair of Marks and Sparks knicks – I know because I nearly bought the same pattern for Gretchen. As I think about it, a lump comes to my throat – which is something that lumps seem to have a habit of doing in this cabin. There is no doubt about it but that Muna is a right cracker and I salute the fact by slipping off the bunk and rising to the majestic vertical before taking her in my arms. I kiss her hair and then her here, and then her here and her there, and slip my hands inside her panties so that her back bumpers are nestling comfortably against my hands like a couple of pumpkins that might fall off the back of the lorry. It is funny but she is not what you might call a passionate kisser when working on the mouth feature. Quite reserved in fact. I believe they are a bit like that once you get across the foothills of the Himalayas. Discreet in the obvious bits but deliciously dirty once the sound of the temple bells has been muffled by the falling mosquito nets.

My hampton is still raking the sky like it is waiting for unidentified aircraft and I give Muna's muff fluff a tickle and send the filthy five for a ramble through happy valley.

'Let's get on the floor,' I say. OK, so it's not the most sophisticated approach since 'All About Eve' but it does make the point and avoid any risk of confusion. If I said to this chick, 'Shall we measure our lengths against the Axminster?' she would probably start looking around for a tape measure.

My message is clearly understood but Muna settled on the carpet in a sitting position and not in the standard backs to the land, 'Me Jane, you Tarzan,' east to west position beloved by generations of British in and out specialists. She smiles up at me and stretches out a hand and I shed my threads and squat on the carpet facing her. I suppose it saves your knees, doesn't it? No sooner have I alighted than she shuffles forward and throws her legs over my thighs. In this position, my Mad Mick is closer to her snatch than a screw to a washer and it requires but a little wriggle and an adjustment of the angle of rake before happy Perce has plunged into the velvet gloaming. It is not at all unpleasant because I am now face to face with the bird and we can indulge in a bit of kissing and touching without getting belter's elbow. I would not call it a passionate position but it is better than sitting with a stuffed crocodile on your lap. Muna starts to rock backwards and forwards whilst running her fingers up and down my chest – plus a lot of other places – and I get the feeling that her kick is giving me kicks. She watches my every reaction very carefully and makes turning-on purring noises. This kind of treatment does not take long to get through to you and I soon feel like a volcano when it knows it is going to have one of its turns. A trickle turns into a tremble that becomes a shiver which builds up to a sensation which makes me grab Muna to me and take control of the rocking motion that is binding us together. She fits my body as if sculpted to it and lets out a long low moan at the same time shoving her hand beneath my legs to 'milk' my cobblers. It is what you might call affecting and I have less chance of stopping myself coming than I have of preventing Shrove Tuesday following Monday.

'Oh!' I gasp. 'That's – OOH!'

It is at this inconvenient moment that there is a sharp rap on the door and I hear Sid's voice. 'Timmo! Are you in there?'

'Yes!' I grunt.

'Well, come on then. Let's be having you!'

'Right, Sid.' With a sigh of release, I do as my brother-in-law suggests.

CHAPTER FOUR

In which Timmy starts off on the wrong foot and locates some marmalade for excitable Mrs Reynolds.

'In the old days, I'd have had you keel hauled,' says Pervis. 'Your flabby bodies would have been scraping the barnacles off the hull.'

'That's not very nice,' says Sid. 'We came on board in good faith, trying to help you out. You'd be two stewards short if it wasn't for us. Frankly, I'm amazed at your attitude. What about the dignity of labour? All this Mutiny on the Bounty stuff doesn't belong in the twentieth century.'

Personally, I think that Sid is coming it a bit strong and there is little doubt that Purser Pervis agrees. He has a face that looks as if the last vestiges of human feeling were scraped off it with a rusty razor blade and I do not care for the five little balls he is running through his fingers. When he looks at us I get the feeling that he would like four more to make up the set.

'Don't think you can blackmail me, you son of a sea cook,' he snarls. 'I could still have you slapped in irons as a couple of stowaways.'

'The Captain might have something to say about that,' says Sid.

'The Captain wouldn't care if I put you through the bacon slicer for the crew's sandwiches!' says Pervis. 'I'm in charge around here and you'd better remember that. I tell the Captain what I've done, I don't ask him. He drives the ship. I look after the passenger staff.'

'I'm sorry if we jumped the gun,' I say, flashing on the

wholesome smile that I use to dazzle old ladies and traffic wardens – often the same people. 'When our friends went down with food poisoning we thought we were doing the right thing.'

'Don't simper at me, you half wit!' snaps Pervis. 'You step out of line and I'll lock you up. You're on probation as far as I'm concerned. I'll be watching you very carefully. Report to Seaman Blout, he'll put you to work.'

'What a pretty name,' says Sid.

'We should never have given ourselves up,' I say, as we go through the door. 'He nearly chucked us in the chokey, didn't he?'

'I was half hoping he would,' says Sid. 'Anything to get away from Muna. She's a lovely girl but she does crowd a two berth cabin.'

'She tried to placate you again, did she, Sid?' I ask.

'She never stops,' says Sid. 'You know what it's like. She whips it out like it's the only thermometer in a flu epidemic.'

Sid certainly has a point – but only just. Muna is more than generous with the love interest and your trousers are not the only things it gets down after a while. I like a spot of in and out as much as the next man but there are times when even an excitable youth craves to be left alone with his Hugo's 'Teach yourself Spanish' in readiness to challenge life's wider frontiers. SS *Tern* is on a cruise of the Mediterranean and I am looking forward to getting ashore and conversing with the locals in their native tongue. Now that we are well and truly in the Common Market, it behoves each and every one of us to be able to say 'Go home, wogs!' in at least half a dozen different languages.

When we come into the presence of Seaman Blout it is to find him apparently trying to push a hole in the side of the ship. His body looks as if someone squeezed it so tightly round the middle that all the flesh fled to his thighs and shoulders and it is not difficult to perceive that muscle-building has taken place.

'Blimey,' says Sid. 'The last bloke I saw looking like that was trying to wank his way into the Guinness Book of Records. What's up, mate?'

'Isometric training,' grunts the geezer, gritting his teeth and giving the bulkhead a last savage thrust.

'You's a whatsit?' says Sid.

'It's a way of building up muscle by pushing against inanimate objects,' I say. I would not admit this to just anybody but I once had a bash at turning myself into 'Mr Clapham' myself. I bought a book called 'How I built my Cannonball Deltoids' and a sort of chest expander that nearly sawed off my nipples when I closed it a bit sharpish. I remember how the instructions told me that I was going to have 'Herculean power, sculptured muscle, waistline perfection, yard-wide shoulders, jet-powered legs and a wrestler-sized neck.' In fact, the only thing I got was a groin strain that worried me for a few days and a bill for ten quid that worried me for somewhat longer. I was a mug to go in for it because it was about the time that all the birds were going for seven stone weaklings and Charles Atlas was a closed book.

'You too can have a body like mine,' says Blout proudly.

'Uum,' says Sid. 'Well, I suppose it pulls the birds.'

Blout's face clouds over immediately. 'Women, you mean?' he says like one has mentioned slugs. 'They make you weak.'

I have not met a great many crew members of the good ship *Tern* but it does seem that they are not devotees of stabbing the furburger.

'They make my week, all right,' says Sid with a light laugh. 'Right, my muscly matelot. Introduce us to the mysteries of your craft.'

'Are you taking the piss?' says Blout after some thought.

'Not so you ought to be noticing,' says Sid. 'Got a few breakfast trays for late risers? I've a lovely sense of balance.'

'Save it in case Pervis makes you walk the plank,' says Blout sending an ostrich egg for a stroll up and down his arm. 'Yuk yuk, yuk.'

'What do you want us to do?' says Sid, sounding peeved the moment Blout moves in on the funnies.

'Start cleaning out the cabins,' says Blout. 'I'll tell you where to find the stuff. You, Skinny—' he is talking to me, would you believe? 'You got A Deck, fifteen to twenty and twenty-three to twenty-eight.'

'What happened to twenty-one and twenty-two?' I ask.

'They were sold,' says Blout. He goes on to explain that when stewards are issued with a list of cabins at the beginning of a trip they sell them off amongst themselves in expectation of the tip they are likely to get at the end of the voyage.

'But how could Smallwood sell them when he wasn't here?' I ask.

'I did it for him,' says Blout.

'And who bought them?'

'I did,' says Blout.

'I bet you paid a very reasonable price,' says Sid. 'Right, let's get on with it. I knew I'd be sailing under the Red Duster but this is ridiculous.'

I am chuffed to bollocks to get somewhere where there is a chance of seeing the sea. So far I have not even clocked it out of a porthole. My dreams of lounging around amongst the frippet on the passenger decks are well and truly up the spout. Apparently, we are not allowed to fraternise with the paying customers and even the ship's officers are supposed to retire to their cabins by eleven o'clock if not on duty. Working below decks is like slaving in a steel rabbit warren and I reckon the job has about as much glamour as being an air hostess – or stewardess as you have to call them if you don't want a clip round the earhole. As for the food, well it is diabolical, even worse than the stuff the customers are expected to eat. And there is no booze, either. It is not surprising that most of the stewards are gingers. No girls, no gargle and scampering up and down narrow corridors at all hours of the day and night. It must give you a passage complex, mustn't it?

When I decide that I can't stand being cooped up any longer I take a tray and walk round the deck with it. This does mean that a few old geezers start ordering whisky sours and the like but I just listen politely and then go on my way never to be seen again. I am expecting to stumble across the fair Caroline almost immediately but the ship is so chocker that it is not until we are in the middle of the Bay of Biscay that the magic moment occurs. This Bay of Biscay feature is definitely a choppy one and, on the morning in question, quite a few of the passengers are indulging in a liquid laugh over the side of the vessel. It is definitely a time to keep your porthole bolted. Fortunately for the future of the British Empire and Solihull, the Rankins are made of sterner stuff and as I come round the corner it is to find Caroline struggling with a deck chair whilst the *Tern* lurches through thirty degrees and spray occasionally breaks over the decks. Mum and Dad are sitting in wicker chairs with blankets over their laps and looking like they passed away during the night. This is clearly where I make up for my tiny lapse with the cabin trunk.

'Good morning!' I say briskly. 'Bit fresh today, isn't it? Still, it blows away the cobwebs, I suppose. Can I give you a hand with that?'

I don't wait for an answer but grab the deck chair and swing it round so that I can get to grips with it. It is of course cruel, bad luck that at that precise moment a vicious squall fills the canvas and suddenly turns it into a sail that propels me towards Mr Rankin. I see his eyes widen in recognition and horror half a second before I sprawl across his lap and get the deck chair hooked over his head.

'I'm sorry!' I screech. 'I'll just – oh.'

I swing the deck chair round and bash Mrs Rankin on the side of the bonce. Oh dear, I can feel that this is going to be one of my mornings.

'Yaarrrrgh!' The ship gives a terrifying lurch and I stagger backwards across the slippery decks. The deck chair is held above my head and as my back whacks against the rail I release my hold and the killer canvas sails into the ocean.

'Good God! The man's insane.' Rankin sinks back in his seat and his wife pulls her blanket up under her chin.

'It's the wind,' I shout. Desperate to make amends, I pull at a pile of deck chairs that spill across the deck. An invalid chair is moored behind them and this glides away gathering speed until it catches up with a steward carrying a tray of drinks. He is swept up, still holding his tray, and dashed against the rail at the end of the deck. The tray sails over the edge and there are screams and angry shouts from below.

'Please don't bother!' says Caroline. 'I'd rather do it myself.'

I am now standing inside a deck chair with one of the

wooden bits over my shoulder and the canvas between my legs. God knows how I got like that. Usually it does not take me more than half an hour to put up a deck chair.

'Give me another one,' I say. 'This one's a bit stiff.'

'Come away from him, Caroline!' squeaks Mrs Rankin. Stupid old bag, she is beginning to get on my nerves.

'I'm only trying to help,' I say.

'Please don't,' begs Mrs Rankin. 'Please go away and leave us in peace.'

'What are you doing here, Lea?' The voice is the sole property of Purser Pervis and the smarmy expression on his mug is draining away faster than love juice at a pop festival.

'I'm just putting up a deck chair, sir,' I say.

'You look as if you're putting it up your jacksy!' hisses Pervis. 'Get out of it and get below. You're not supposed to be up here.'

'Right, sir. Sorry, sir. If you'll just hold my – oops!' It is very unfortunate that the geezer with the tray of coffees comes on deck just as Pervis savagely wrenches the deck chair off my foot and catches him in the cobblers with the back swing. He collapses to his knees with an oath and as Pervis snatches up the tray with a speed and agility that would be the envy of any English slip fielder, the ship gives another lurch and Mr Rankin cops the lot in his lap. I don't catch exactly what he says but it does seem that for once the coffee is hot.

I don't hang around to receive apologies but bid a swift farewell to Caroline and leg it back to the underworld.

'Where have you been?' says Blout, pressing a couple of rivets through the wall with his little finger. 'There's a dirty breakfast tray outside one two five. Get on to it.'

'Should I take the plate off first?' I say. 'I don't want to break anything.'

It is clear that Blout has not warmed to my sunny nature. 'You want to watch it,' he says. 'Mr Pervis has got it in for you.'

'That's very nice of him,' I say. 'But I can usually get it in for myself.'

When I pad round to one two five it is to find that a very comely redhead from one two six is bending over the tray. She is wearing a black net robe and her cleft back bumpers look like a ripe peach. I clock their inviting fullness and feel Percy emit a Tarzan yodel from the depths of the pubic jungle. Of course, I am deeply in love with Caroline Rankin but that is no reason why I cannot pay respectful homage to the beauty of an udder – I mean, another. It must have been seeing her knockers that made me say that. When she stands up and brushes the barnet from her mince pies I am reminded of a couple of pouter pigeons ruffling their feathers at the mouth of the dovecote –you can call me nature boy if you like.

'Oh,' she says. 'I was just seeing if there was any Golden Shred. The perennial myrtle becomes a trifle tedious, doesn't it?'

'Definitely,' I say, wondering what she is on about. Then I see that she has picked up one of the little containers of jam that are dished out on the breakfast trays. 'Oh,' I say. 'You haven't had it yet – I mean, the breakfast?' I add the last bit when she gives me a funny look.

'I would love a spot of marmalade,' she says. 'Could you be a poppet and lay hands on some for me?'

'Of course,' I say. 'I'll nip round to the pantry and see what we've got.'

The pantry is the posh name for the place where the

blue-bottles go to be seasick and I am surprised to find that there is a stack of marmalade there.

'You want to put some more of this out,' I say. 'There's a big demand for it.'

One of the cooks looks at me like I am round the twist. 'You must be new around here,' he says. 'The whole idea is to keep a few items in short supply. When people ask for them you say "Ooh, dodgy, guv'nor. I'll try but I can't promise nothing". When you turn up with the stuff, they think you're a bleeding marvel and you cop a bigger tip at the end of the trip. It's simple psychology, see?'

It occurs to me, as I scamper back along the companionway, that there are few men on the up and up aboard the good ship *Tern* and that a young innocent boy needs to keep his wits about him lest he fall into unwholesome ways. I tap discreetly on the door of one two six and am bade enter by a voice that sounds like honey being poured over warm treacle. The nice redheaded lady is lying on top of her bed and her eyes light up when she sees my tiny offering.

'Don't say you've done it?' she husks. 'That is wonderful. You are clever.'

I think she is overdoing it a bit and I can't help blushing. 'Have you got everything else you need?' I say. 'All right for toast, are you?'

'Fine, thank you. It's such a good way to use up the stale bread, isn't it? If I can just get this top off.' She starts picking at the foil with her enormous scarlet talons and I stretch out my hand.

'Shall I have a go?'

'Oh would you? I'm certain you've got the knacker.' And the moment she says that she runs her hand up my thigh as if determined to find out. What a funny woman!

'Eer – can I borrow your knife?'

'Why, do you think you might have to protect yourself?' She smiles up at me and then starts buttering a piece of toast that is trying to touch its toes.

I don't think she expects an answer to that so I slip the knife under the foil tab and peel back the lid of the container.

'There we are.' Using all my considerable powers of muscular dexterity and physical co-ordination, I manage to hand over the marmalade without spilling a single bit down the front of her bristols. Quite an achievement I am certain you will agree – especially as my mince pies are glued to the fun feature as if by a powerful adhesive.

'Well,' I say, a note of lingering regret entering my voice. 'That's – er it, then. Bon uppertits – I mean, appetit.' Blast! I should never have tried that fancy French bit. That is what comes of watching only two episodes of 'Parlez-vous français?' on the telly and not sending off for the booklet. I could be so suave if I persevered.

'Thank you.' The lady looks down at her Manchesters and in so doing manages to drop a dab of freshly spread marmalade at the head of the valley that allows her a sight of her belly button without overstretching her bushel. Whilst I watch entranced, the marmalade slowly slides from view.

'Clumsy me.' The redhead gives a delicious wriggle and her eyes meet mine. 'Could you pass me those tissues, please?' She puts the toast back on the plate and wriggles her fingers. 'That's the trouble with breakfast in bed. It's so messy, isn't it? Crumbs everywhere and sticky fingers.'

I pass her the tissues and she takes one and wipes her fingers on it. I have never seen a woman who makes every gesture seem as if it has something to do with sex. 'Perhaps it would be better if you had a go?' And, so help me, she only claps her hands on her boobs and pulls them apart, doesn't she? 'Do you mind?'

'Er – oh, no. Of course not.' I fold a tissue in half and steer my mit towards the half inch of dessicated orange peel that is wedged in the fissure between the two noble knockers. Gosh! I certainly cop the tough assignments, don't I?

'Why don't you wipe it on him?' For a moment I wonder what she is on about. Then I follow her eyes. She is gazing at the spot where my snatch scratcher stirs restlessly behind the restraining denim like a tiger stalking backwards and forwards across its cage.

'Do you want to lose me my job?' I say.

'Not particularly,' purrs the redheaded flesh fiend. 'I just want to extend your role – amongst other things.' She presses her head against my thigh and nuzzles me in the nadgers. This is disgusting. I would not believe it if I was reading about it in one of those library books that is always out when you want it and comes back with the pages stuck together.

'Mrs – er—'

'Reynolds. Lock the door and come to bed with me. I feel in the mood for an impulsive adventure.' I look down at the tray and she shoves it into my hands. 'Come on. What have you got to be frightened of?'

'Nothing really,' I say. 'I'm just a bit surprised, that's all. I haven't had much experience of life at sea.'

'Well, come on board and I'll give you some.' Mrs Reynolds grits her teeth and starts tugging at my belt. When that pops open she sucks in her breath and puts both hands on the top of my jeans. 'Going down,' she coos. Men's underwear, cucumbers . . .' Percy pops out like a drawbridge on elastic chains and Mrs Reynolds seizes him like she is scared he might shake free of his mooring.

'Welcome, stranger,' she breathes. 'Get the rocks out of your socks and let's probe for the missing marmalade.'

'Well – er, right!' I say – I mean, you just can't turn that kind of offer down, can you? Not without giving offence and that is the last thing I want to do. Mrs Reynolds releases her hold on my hampton and cases my joints whilst I shed my threads like a snake watching dinner approaching. At last – well, would you believe fifteen and a half seconds later? – I am standing there, naked as nature intended. And when I say standing, I mean standing. The wicked winkle is rearing up like a great dane on tiptoe.

'Superyum!' husks Mrs Reynolds wriggling down her bed. 'Let's play an updated version of "fifteen men on a dead man's chest".' She slaps her hands round her bristols and pushes them up towards her chin. 'Can you see the marmalade?'

'I can see a bit of peel,' I say.

'Well, come and get it!' She keeps her hands on her bristols and whips them apart in what might be considered an inviting gesture. Can it really be that the lady wishes me to—?

Ah well, there seems only one way to find out. As Mrs Reynolds hurls aside the sheet that covers her lower limbs, I scramble across her Derby Kell so that my orchestras are hatching her belly button and my Molly O'Morgan is dead on line for her top bollocks. In this position, harm can come to a young girl but Mrs Reynolds shows no signs of fear.

'Advance and be recognised,' she trills, once more laying hands on the purple-headed bed snake.

Eager not to disappoint, I shuffle up the lady's torso

whilst she waits with her hands on her Manchesters like they are a couple of flesh cymbals waiting for the right bar to arrive – and there are no prizes for guessing which is the right bar as far as Mrs Reynolds is concerned.

'Got you!' she breathes. 'Oooh, that's lovely! I can feel its ribs.' I think she exaggerates but I am in no mood to argue with her. When she turns your giggle stick into the filling in a knocker sandwich it is inclined to take your mind off things.

'Look at his little red head peeping out,' she coos. 'He looks like a monk in a cowl.' I had never thought of it like that myself, but I suppose it is a question of how you look at things. 'Let's see if we've located that marmalade.' She releases Percy and looks between her bristols. 'It's not there so it must be – ah, yes.' Her eyes travel the length of my hampton and then widen in pleasure. 'Here we are.' She slips her hands behind my back and urges me up her body until there is nowhere left for Percy to go except the strip of velvet heaven guarded by her rose hips.

I let her enjoy her breakfast the way she clearly likes it and tilt my body and hand back so that I can give her spasm chasm a friendly tickle. Talk about Eel Pie Island. Mrs Reynolds is clearly ready for a grumble rumble and I wonder which way to turn. If I stay where I am much longer, I won't have a choice. Fortunately, Mrs Reynolds decides that she has had enough marmalade-flavoured cock for one morning and indicates that the mighty wurlitzer can thump out love's sweet melody in another quarter.

'Oh,' she breathes as Percy goes berserk in her melody box. 'How lovely to find a steward who isn't bent.'

CHAPTER FIVE

In which Janice and Anthea combine to extend our hero in their search for things to do on board.

The trouble with Mrs Reynolds – well, one of the troubles – is that she has so many friends. That same evening, when I am turning down the beds in one two eight, a bird comes in wearing a long towelling robe. That is all very well but when she takes it off she has nothing on underneath it.

'It's all right,' she says. 'I'm a friend of Kate's. I don't shock easily.'

'Kate?' I say.

'Kate Reynolds. You served her this morning in one two six.'

'Oh yes,' I say, trying not to look at the bits where the delicious brown turns into tempting white. 'Well, have a nice evening. I believe there's bingo in First Class.'

'I'm more interested in bung-ho than bingo,' says the bird gazing deep into my fickle brown eyes.

'How about a film, then?' I say. 'I can't remember what it's called. Something about a Pop Performer. They had it on Wednesday and I believe it's very . . .' My voice drifts away as the bird squirts some cream on to her hand with a naughty noise and starts massaging it into her shapely bristols.

'Do you like the perfume?'

'Very – er nice,' I say, watching how the nipples are beginning to stand out brown and shiny.

'What else can you recommend?'

'I dunno,' I say. 'There's always something going on.

You know, there's that notice outside the purser's office.' I wince when I think of Pervis because I have been keeping one step ahead of him all day. I believe that he wants to see me and I don't reckon it is because he wishes to congratulate me on my hospital corners. 'Anyway, I'd better be going. I'd hate your old man to come back and get the wrong idea.'

I nod towards the other bed in the room but Shiny Knockers shakes her head. 'That's not my husband,' she says. 'I'm travelling with my girlfriend. We're schoolteachers from Barnstaple.'

'Lovely part of the world,' I say. 'Well, enjoy yourselves.'

I had intended these to be my final words but the lady has positioned herself between me and the door. 'I hope its going to look up a bit,' she says. 'We're both finding it rather flat at the moment. Not what we expected at all. No high jinks.'

Her bristols give a little bounce on the word 'jinks' and she must see my eyelids flutter. 'You know what I mean, don't you? We thought we'd be able to let our hair down.'

'There's the fancy dress ball,' I say. 'I believe that's always a highlight.'

The truth is that Muna started showing her gratitude in traditional Pakistani style at dinner time and I am just the teeniest bit knackered. You can't put it about all the time and maintain the same level of appetite.

'I was thinking of something a little less organised than that,' says the bird. 'Something completely impromptu. Surely there must be occasions when you find yourself in a compromising position with a woman who clearly has only one thing on her mind?'

'You mean, like now when you've just shoved your hand

down the front of my trousers?' I say. 'Yes, now you come to mention it, funny things do happen sometimes.'

'I don't know what's come over me,' says the bird as I look down nervously. 'Maybe it's the ozone.'

'I'm not wearing any,' I say. Just goes to show, doesn't it? I always thought those after-shave advertisements were a load of cobblers but they obviously stir up the birds by some kind of auto-suggestion.

'I didn't mean that,' says the bird, bestowing an impassioned wriggle upon my chest feature. 'OooH!!' She submerges my north and south in cakehole and it is clear that an element of frustration has crept into her nature. Oh dear, what am I going to do? If only Percy was not passion's plaything and could conduct himself with the glacial restraint that characterises the rest of my nature. On occasions like this I feel that we are two different people and that he only hangs around because he finds it warm between my thighs. Somebody who would probably not argue with him is the lady currently engaged in harvesting my nuts.

'Oh,' she pants. 'Please don't go. Oh!' If she is talking to proud Percy she need have no fears. This lad hangs about like fog on the set of a Hollywood movie featuring London.

'Please!' I say. 'These trousers are cut on the tight side and you could ruin your watch face on the inside of my zip.'

It is becoming clear to me that there is only one way to escape from this situation. The girl will go into a swift decline if I don't give her one and she is supposed to be on holiday. Kindness demands that I do the decent thing – e.g. the indecent thing. Injecting some menace into the motion of my molars I overrun her cakehole and swiftly expose Percy to the worst that she has to offer. Whilst she fondles my orchestras, I tiptoe into Glen Love-it and frisk amongst the foliage for a few seconds before dunking my digits in her joint-anointer. This is clearly a moving experience as far as she is concerned because she shudders like Harold Wilson looking at the latest trade figures and renews her attempts to put her head inside my mouth. If I did not know that she was a schoolteacher I would think that she ran a wild animal act. Sensing that a desire for coition is somewhat nearer than the back of her mind, I pop my mits under her sit feature and bunk her up my body so that my Mad Mick is quivering at the entrance of her pleasuredrome.

'Yes!' she breathes. '*Yes!*'

She manoeuvres the magic morsel to the spot where it can do the most damage and slides down six inches of ecstasy with a sound like your Aunty Flo easing herself into a hot bath. She is now firmly established upon the magic poundabout and I stagger forward hampered by the trousers flapping round my knees. Five paces to the bed and I topple forward, lucky to end up with no more than a crinkle in my winkle at the moment of impact. After all the flesh gargles I have enjoyed lately it makes a change to get back to straightforward in and out and I release Percy like he is zooming out of the barrel of a twenty-five pounder.

'Oh!' gasps my new playmate. 'Ow! WOW!!'

I am so deeply involved in what I am doing that I don't hear the door opening behind me. 'Anthea! Is it anyone I know?'

I nearly jump out of her skin when I hear the voice but Anthea has a grip of steel when it comes to missing out on the balaclava and promptly thrusts me in again. 'I don't think so,' she grunts. 'Kate Reynolds put me on to him.'

'It doesn't look as if she needed a crane,' says the new bird drily.

'Do shut the door, Janice,' gasps Anthea. 'Anyone might come.'

I am inclined to agree with her, putting myself forward as a strong contender for an early wack-off. It is funny how some birds draw like a well-built chimney, isn't it? This one builds up so much suction that I can feel my orchestras straining at their moorings.

I am not really concentrating but I can't help hearing the door slam and a sound like that of someone shedding their these and those. I turn my head and – oh gawd! Janice is practically down to her suntan. There is an anticipatory smile on her face like she has got half a water melon in her cakehole and she has just torn one of her fingernails ripping off her knicks.

'Girls!' I say. 'Seriously. Is this a good idea?' I am a mug to open my mouth because that is the kind of question that nobody ever answers and I don't have the strength to waste on buckshee words.

Janice's knockers alight on the small of my back like birds of passage – no, not that one – and her wicked looks and lingers perform an erotic Pawnee – or should it be porny? – fertility dance round the base of my scrotum pole.

'Come on, Anthea!' she urges. 'We said we'd go half shares in everything on this holiday, remember.'

'You'll have to talk to her about your share if you don't stop doing that,' I say. 'Oooh!'

'Stop interfering with him!' say Anthea, trying to slap Janice's mits away and catching me an unhelpful one in the cobblers in the process. 'First come, first served.'

'And first served, first come,' I gasp. 'Yowee! Blast off!' They have forced me to use the ultimate deterrent – post orgasmic wilting willy. I don't like to have to do it but I can't go on like a worm being tugged apart by a couple of sparrows. A man can only take – and give – so much.

'Thank you, girls,' I gasp. 'That was – yes!' My face nosedives into a pillow and I try and suck in breath.

'What about me?' says Janice.

'You were great,' I croak. 'I couldn't have done it without you.'

'Anthea! Has he—?'

'Yes, dear. I'm afraid so.'

Janice chokes back a sob. 'How thoughtless. What am I going to do?'

'Don't worry,' says Anthea calmly. 'We'll just have to wait until it gets better. Help me push the chest-of-drawers in front of the door.'

I think it is the 'we' that worries me most.

CHAPTER SIX

In which Timmy and Sid find the job getting on top of them and are forced to take unusual measures to avoid the attentions of man-hungry passengers.

'I've just declared my crutch a disaster area,' says Sid. 'I wonder if I could apply for Government aid?'

'I know what you mean, Sid,' I say. 'Just a jar of Vaseline wouldn't go down amiss.'

'It would probably go up a miss, knowing you,' says Sid. He looks at me expectantly and then shrugs his shoulders. 'Yeh, I know what you mean. It's no laughing matter, is it? If we don't get away from these birds we're going to be able to flog our tonks as pyjama cord tassles. What gets into them when they get to sea?'

'Only you and me, that's the trouble,' I say. 'We're not getting any help from the rest of the crew. They're gingers to a man and bugger all use to a woman. And having Muna in the cabin doesn't help. You'll have to speak to her, Sid.'

'It's difficult with her mouth always full,' says Sid. 'I've never been able to hold a conversation like that.'

'I wonder how easy it is to let one of those lifeboats down,' I say thoughtfully.

'Funny you should mention that,' says Sid. 'I was having a crafty drag the other day and this bloke stuck his head out from underneath the tarpaulin and asked me if I'd got a ham sandwich on me.'

'Stowaway, was he?'

'No. Apparently, he was a waiter suffering from the same problem as ourselves. They used to come and drag him out of his bunk. In the end he decided he couldn't take any more, and he's been hiding in a lifeboat for days. As soon as we get close enough to shore he's going to swim for it.'

'What about sharks?'

'He wasn't worried. He said that after what he'd been through, sharks would be like Yorkshire terriers.'

'Oh my gawd. What are we going to do, Sid?'

Before Sid can open his cakehole, the cabin door bursts open and Pervis strides in with Seaman Blout at his elbows – Blout is so wide that he is behind both of them. 'Got you!' he snarls. 'Report to my cabin in five minutes or I'll have your giblets swinging from the yardarm.'

'How messy,' says Sid.

'What's this?' Pervis picks up one of Muna's saris – luckily the lady has nipped off to make herself a curry butty, or whatever. 'Just like the rest of them, are you?'

'It's a phase I'm going through,' I say. 'Would you like to see my sitar?'

'Watch your language in front of Mr Pervis,' says Blout.

'Four and a half minutes!' hisses Pervis. He takes a last look round the cabin like it is a blown-up photograph of a flea's crutch and goes out with Blout trying to judge the distance so that he can get his shoulders through the door-way without damaging the metal.

'The most menacing duo since Shirley Temple bought her first bra,' says Sid. 'What do you think he wants us for?'

'Maybe Smallwood and his mate have put the fuzz on to us,' I say.

Sid adapts his George Raft sneer and nonchalantly tosses a coin into the air. You scare too easily,' he says.

I pick up the coin and hand it back to him. 'Come on,' I say. 'We'd better not be late.'

Purser Pervis's office betrays his nautical bent with pictures on the wall that have names like 'Off Valparaiso'. They show sailing boats that look like your mum's laundry about to blow off the line and dipping into the briny at an angle of forty-five degrees. I don't have time to tell Pervis how much I like them because he starts doing his nut the minute we get through the door.

'Right! you scum,' he snarls. 'Don't say I didn't warn you. It was only with the greatest reluctance that I didn't clap you in irons when you first tried to blackmail me into giving you a job. You have betrayed my trust.'

'I didn't know you wore one,' says Sid. 'What are you raving about? I thought you'd brought us here to promote us.'

'Mr Rankin is threatening to sue for the damage he suffered at your hands Lea. I suppose you realise that he's big in P & O?'

'He did niff a bit, now you come to mention it,' I say.

'I said P & O, not B O!' raps Pervis.

'What have I done?' says Sid.

'Mrs Brewster has complained that you attacked her last night.'

'She didn't complain when I was doing it,' says Sid. 'She's just narky because I wouldn't give in to her disgusting demands. Fourteen times in one night should be enough for any woman.'

'Are you prepared to stand by that?' I ask.

'Not after doing it fourteen times,' said Sid.

'Shut up!' screams Pervis. 'When I want to listen to terrible jokes I'll go to the ship's concert party.'

'Sounds groovy,' says Sid. 'Will you sit next to me?'

'I'll buy the ice creams,' I say.

Pervis grits his teeth so hard that I will swear I can see sparks flying out of his cakehole. 'I'm going to lock you up,' he hisses. 'And when we get to Gibraltar I'm going to hand you over to the British authorities.'

'What will they do with us?' says Sid.

'I don't know,' says Pervis. 'But if you find yourself sitting on a bloody great rock with fifteen other apes, don't be surprised!' I am about to ask for further details when the telephone rings. Pervis snatches it up and his mug goes all smooth and haughty. 'Purser speaking.' He listens for a moment and then quickly puts his hand over the mouthpiece. 'Somebody complaining about their steward,' he says nodding at us meaningfully. I rack my brains and try and suss who it could be. I suppose it was a bit silly to have used that bird's powder puff to clean round the toilet. 'You want *who*?' Pervis's shriek drags me back to the present. 'Are you sure about that, Mrs Reynolds?' I feel a sudden pang of fear as if I had just stepped into a compartment full of Manchester United supporters after a home defeat by Crewe Alexandra. 'Lea?' Pervis looks at me and then back into the mouthpiece like he can't believe his bottles. 'Are you sure? Yes, of course, it is possible. Yes, well, if you're quite certain, Mrs Reynolds.'

Sid rubs his hands together and gives me a nudge. 'That's you up the Khyber, matey. Three months hard, that's what you've got to look forward to.'

'Right,' says Pervis, shaking his head as he puts the phone down. 'You can add one two six to your rota, Lea. Don't expect me to be so lenient in future.'

'I don't want leniency!' I yelp. 'I'll take what's coming to me like a man.'

'Exactly,' says Sid. 'Don't try and wriggle out of it when Mr Pouve has shown you the forgiving side of his nature.'

Before Pervis can say anything, the phone rings again. 'Hello, Purser speaking. Oh yes. How are you, Mrs Brewster? Recovered from your ordeal? Good. Yes, I've got him in front of me as a matter of fact. I'm just going to see that he – *What*? You want to give him another chance?'

'Lock me up!' screams Sid shoving both wrists across the desk. 'Where's the nick? I'll do it myself!'

'Shut up!' says Pervis, putting down the phone and leaning back in his swivel chair. 'You obviously satisfy some need too horrible to think about, and since the motto of Splendormed Cruises is "The Customer Comes First", you had better continue to ensure that this is always the case. Do I make myself clear?'

'You're sentencing us to death!' sobs Sid. 'Have you no spark of human decency?'

'None,' says Pervis. 'I'm only sorry that I can't punish you in a more traditional manner – spreadeagled across the rigging and flogged with a cat of nine tails.'

After Pervis has finished proving that he is just an old romantic at heart, Sid and I tiptoe out into the companionway. Aptly named it is, too, because a couple of companions swing round the corner before we can hit the stairs. Anthea and Janice as I live and breathe nervously.

'Ah, room service,' says Anthea cheerfully. 'Just what I need. Steer a couple of highballs round to our cabin, will you, steward?'

'Let's make it a round four,' purrs Janice. 'And they don't have to be all that high.'

'Stone the crows!' says Sid when the birds have disappeared, saying that they will expect us in five minutes. 'Do you think there's any more room in that geezer's lifeboat?'

'And you said that this was going to be a rest cure,' I accuse. 'Next time I want a rest I'll lend my balls to a driving range.'

Three quarters of an hour later, I would not be able to

lend them as door stops in a free brothel. The things those birds have done to us should be outlawed by the Geneva Convention.

'Sid,' I gasp. 'We can't go on like this. We'll be gonners in a couple of days.'

'I've got it,' says Sid.

'Oh no!' I say. 'That's all we need. Have you seen the MO? Maybe it's only—'

'I didn't mean that!' says Sid. 'It's what Pervis said when he saw Muna's sari that gave me the idea.'

'You mean when he thought we were bent?'

'Exactly. We've got to make a few more people think that. The rest of the crew don't have any problems, do they?'

'But they *are* bent.'

'I'm not suggesting we go the whole hog,' says Sid. 'The only passage round the Mediterranean I intend to work is my own. What I'm saying is that we should camp it up a bit so that the birds leave us alone. We can borrow some of Muna's make-up, she won't mind.'

'I don't want to wear make-up,' I say.

'Just a bit of eye shadow,' says Sid breezily. 'It might suit you. Bring out a few hidden highlights.'

Well, I hate to admit this, but Sid is right. It is amazing what lovely cheekbones I have. I had never noticed it before. And my eyes. They are like limpid pools once you get a bit of boot polish over the lids. Only the lipstick is a disappointment. I mean, it tastes so diabolical. They ought to make one flavoured with mild and bitter.

'This could save our lives,' says Sid as we take a shufti at our made-up mugs in the mirror. 'That and Muna getting off at Gibraltar. She's a lovely girl but I won't be sorry to see the back of her.'

'I don't think I've ever seen the back of her,' I say. 'She's always coming at you head first, isn't she?'

'Don't be coarse,' says Sid. 'It doesn't suit the new you.'

One bag of coke who notices the new me immediately is the ginger I bumped into when I first came aboard. 'Oh yes!' he says. 'Definitely. That's what going to sea is all about. Show us your hornpipe.'

'I'll show you a bunch of fives up your bracket,' I say, menacing him with my Oliver Twist. 'Don't get any ideas about me, mate.'

'Promised to another, eh?' simpers the poove. 'I don't know what you see in that Noggett creature. He's so crude.'

'You haven't seen him since he had his hair tinted,' I say.

I mean, honestly, Sid always carries things too far. Give him a good idea and he has to overdo it. I know sailors wear earrings, but not ones that brush against their shoulders. The ones he has got nearly dislodge his shoulder bag.

The first bird to cop my new persona – good word that, isn't it? It's no wonder people tell me that they find these books a proper education – is Mrs Reynolds. When I get to her cabin she is lying on the bed in a diaphanous nightie and showing enough cleavage to prop a plank in.

'Ah,' she says. 'It's Semen Lea. I've forgotten under what implausible pretext I summoned you hither. Never mind. Rid yourself of that unflattering uniform and start shivering my timbers.'

I ignore the lady's outstretched arm and trip lightly to her dressing table. 'Ooh,' I say. 'What a heavenly shade of pink. Do you mind if I try it?' I don't wait for a reply but plonk myself down and start running her lipstick over my rose hips. I can see in the mirror that Mrs Reynolds is worried.

'What's got into you?' she says.

'Ah!' I say. 'That would be telling. No names, no pack drill. Let's just say that I feel a new man – or any man, really. I'm not fussy.' I let my wrist go limper than a piece of wet karsi paper and advance towards the bed. 'Did you want me for something?'

'No!' says Mrs Reynolds, pulling her negligee across her knockers. 'I mean, yes. I'd – er like a pot of tea, please.'

'And one of chef's little cakes?' I say. 'Do try one. He's such a poppet and it will make his day.'

A bit more chat like that and I can see Mrs Reynolds wondering how she ever allowed me to vacuum her bristols with my all forlorn. If I had thought of this caper before, I might never have put my hampton in jeopardy. At least, that is what I think then. But the ways of women are strange, and foolish is he who reckons that what is saucy for the gander is likely to meet with the approval of the National Viewers Council. This I find out when I come across Margaret Uttley and Elisabeth Drake. They are a refined couple of birds and always stuck in a book when I see them. The smallest of them gives me a shy little look from time to time but nothing to make you hang bunting on the front of your Y-fronts. They are looked after by another of the stewards so I don't have anything to do with them until he gets a conan on his fife and goes Uncle Dick. Then I take over. I remember the time well because it is just before we put in at Gibraltar. Sid is thrilled out of his microbe-sized mind because he thinks he is going to start grappling with the mysteries of the magic East and all that rubbish. For him, the Orient begins at Leyton. He is a bit disappointed to find that the first 'bazaar' we go into is called 'The Alhambra Tea Rooms' and is run by a bloke who lived in Shoreditch for thirty years and only went abroad for his wife's health. By the time he has spent the worst part of an hour telling Sid how he yearns to get home again – his wife ran off with a Spaniard after three months but he can't face his old neighbours with the news – I can see my brother-in-law's eyes glazing over, and it is only with the greatest reluctance that he is forced to his fourth cuppa 'on the house' – just as well considering the prices the bloke charges.

'That was a load of laughs,' says Sid when we eventually escape. 'Just our luck to have to bump into him. Where shall we go now?'

'There's the famous brothel quarter,' I say.

'Do me a favour!' says Sid. 'If the girls are relying on me for business, they might as well flog their beds and have a whip round for a knitting machine.'

'Yeh,' I say. 'They wouldn't be very interested in you anyway, would they? Honestly, Sid. You might have taken off your make-up before we came ashore. That's why that bloke was getting so worked up about you. He thought you were going to be a replacement for his old woman.'

'I suppose you're right,' says Sid. 'These heels are a bit high, aren't they?'

'It wouldn't be so bad if they were bloke's shoes,' I say. 'Really, Sid. You do run away with yourself sometimes, which – if I may say so – is more than anyone else would ever do.'

'Shut your face!' says Sid. 'There's no need to be offensive. Any more of that and I'll belt you round the gob with my pearls. That knot can do a bit of damage, you know.'

Eager for a change of subject I cast my eyes about and am surprised to see Miss Uttley and Miss Drake emerging from a dark doorway. There is a furtive expression on their mugs and they are followed by a shifty looking cove resting a hand lightly on Miss Drake's shoulder. Miss Uttley is zipping up her handbag. I would like to probe further into their doings but I don't get the chance because a party of British soldiers come round the corner and try and pick us up. Honestly, they must be desperate for birds in Gibraltar if they want to take Sid dancing. He is so vain that he is actually thinking about going for a minute and in the end they chase us through the Alameda Gardens, up the Grand Parade and three times round the barracks before we can get back to the ship.

'That was a blooming nice afternoon,' pants Sid as we approach our cabin. 'By the cringe! You won't catch me going ashore again. The ship's Chaplain lent me a few dozen copies of the Church Times and I think I'll curl up and do the crosswords. Can you remember what Hezekiah said to the son of Ezekiel?'

Before I can fill Sid in on this surprising lapse in his store of Biblical knowledge I open the door of our cabin and am somewhat taken back by what I see. Muna is lying on the bed wearing a pair of diaphanous pink lounging pants and a warm smile.

'What are you dressed up like that for, gal?' says Sid. 'You can't go ashore in that condition. They lock you up plenty quick quick.' Sid always talks to foreigners like that even when – as in Muna's case – they speak perfect English.

'It's probably because you nicked most of her clobber,' I say. 'The poor kid hasn't got anything left to wear.'

'I no go,' says Muna. 'I think you both lonely without me. Anyway, I no like Gibraltar. I prefer your rocks.'

What can you do in a situation like that? You would have to be heartless not to respond to this girl's simply expressed message of loyalty and affection, wouldn't you? That's what I think anyway. And that's why I step swiftly from the cabin and hang on to the door handle until Sid's screams have turned to whimpers and then to moans. After all, what are friends for?

CHAPTER SEVEN

In which Timmy finds that Elisabeth and Margaret are using him.

When we put to sea, Muna is still with us and Sid is not talking to me – after Muna has finished with him he has difficulty in talking to anyone. I think the noise of the anchor going up made her grit her teeth and there was nearly a nasty accident.

My big moment comes when I bump into Caroline Rankin. She is wearing a little white skirt, gym shoes and socks and looks so wholesome that I would feel guilty taking a bite out of her without cleaning my teeth first. She is carrying a quoit, and tells me that a shower of rain interrupted her game.

'Quoits interruptus,' I say, demonstrating that all those sex books I used to get out of Battersea Public Library have provided me with a rich source of comical quips.

'Ye-es,' she says, eyeing me nervously. 'It was getting a bit blustery, too. Daddy says it's not at all the kind of thing you expect to find in the Med at this time of the year.' She looks at me reproachfully like it was my fault. 'I say, is there anything the matter with your face? It looks as if it's got make-up on it.'

'It's the ship's pantomime,' I say. 'I'm playing Widow Wanky – I mean, Twanky!'

'Oh super!' says Caroline. 'I love pantomimes. Daddy used to take us every Christmas until they got dirty and full of jokes about TV commercials.'

'There's nothing like that in ours,' I assure her. 'There's no hanky panky with my Twanky.'

'Caroline! What are you doing there? It's time to change for dinner.' It is Mrs Rankin, advancing to spoil our love idyll. Just when I was getting into my stride, too. Curses! I hope the soup rots the old bag's dentures.

'I'll see you around,' I murmur, subjecting Caroline to the famous Lea slow burn. 'Perhaps we can get ashore somewhere?'

'Perhaps.' Oh, what a multitude of unspoken promises are contained in that one little word. I am certain that if we could only spend a short time together, something beautiful might emerge.

'Come, Caroline. Remember what your father said.' Mrs Rankin throws me a glance like a hand grenade with the pin missing and steers Caroline out of my life pausing only to say, 'He's queer, dear,' in a voice queerly – I mean clearly – intended for my ears plus those of anybody standing within fifty yards of us.

Queer! How dare she? Clapham's answer to the electric bobbin slighted in this way. I have a good mind to make her eat her words off the end of my hampton. It would probably taste better than the nosh she is going to get in the dining salon, anyway. I watch them disappear, hoping – without success – that Caroline will throw a last glance over her shoulder. Then I go back to my duties. It is tough at the bottom.

I have forgotten about my sighting of Misses Uttley and Drake in swinging downtown Gibraltar but when I am summoned to their cabin it all comes back to me. The air is thick with smoke and its niff is not unknown to me. Pot. Was that what the naughty ladies were spending their pennies on? It certainly seems to have worked a change on the birds for their hair is down – literally – and they are lolling in armchairs wearing flowery print dresses that cover them like patterned dust sheets. I tried pot once but it did nothing for me and the bloke who gave me the joint said that I had to try it a few times to get the full effect. This seemed bloody stupid to me because I thought that pot was something you were supposed to be able to turn on with when you felt like it – like a bit of the other. I am also anti because I don't fancy the idea of smoking. All those ads suggesting that you are likely to get a sexier kind of lung cancer if you smoke Brand X make me sick. Just like the sponsorship of sporting events and pictures of the countryside with fag packets propped up against stooks of corn. OK, so I could take it baked in a cake, but the only person I know who bakes cakes is my Mum and they are deadlier than any drug so far invented.

'Yes, dears?' I say. I have found that calling the female passengers 'dear' is as effective a repellant as telling them that your balls dropped off in the last severe frost.

'You're beautiful!' says Miss Uttley. She starts giggling like a nutter and presses her hand to her mouth.

'Don'tch take any shnotice of sher,' says Miss Drake. 'She's drunk as a ssschkunk.'

'She's trying to suppress my personality,' says the petite Miss Uttley. 'Protect me from her!' So saying, she totters to her feet and throws her arms round my neck. 'You're like a lovely lady,' she says. 'I like you.'

Blast! I must have got lumbered with a couple of David Bowie fans. 'Madam, please!' I lisp. 'Unhand me!'

'Pullsh yourshelf together, Elisabeth. You're making a fool of yourshelf.'

'Shut up, yourshelf, Margaret! You're always saying I'm inhibited.'

Margaret tries to pull Elisabeth off me and the three of us stagger round the floor like an old time medley during ladies' night at the British Legion. 'Please, ladies!' I say. 'State your order or I will have to leave you. I'm serving no useful purpose here.'

'Let's have an orgy, pretty boysy,' says Elisabeth. 'How would you like to suck my joint? Or, better still, why don't I suck—'

'Elisabeth! Control yourshelf.'

'I think I'd better go,' I say, trying to break the head-lock that Elisabeth has on me. The worrying thing is that I am not trying as hard as I ought. There is something rather appealing about young Elisabeth. Something virginal and unsullied that makes me come all over grubby and earthy – not that it probably shows under my Max Factor.

'You mustn't go!' says the bird sounding flatteringly alarmed. 'You're such a pretty man. Not like the others. Don't you find him appealing, Meg?' She takes a deep drag at her joint and flops backwards on to the bed. Ash bounces on to the counterpane and – super servant of Splendormed that I am – I spring forward to dust it to the floor before it can do any damage.

'That's right, Beauty Boy. Come and make love to me.' Elisabeth starts plucking at the buttons of my shirt and I find it difficult to prevent Percy popping up like the finger of a breathed-in rubber glove – it's fun doing that, isn't it? I mean, blowing up inside-out rubber gloves. I also like filling them with water and holding them up my sleeve to shake hands with people. You can end up with a soaking wet armpit and a clip round the earhole from your mum but one must be prepared to suffer for sophisticated amusement.

Anyway, back to the plot. Unless you have just started reading or put the book down to shampoo the canary you will recall that I am kneeling on the bed beside small but beautifully marked Elisabeth Uttley who clearly has designs upon my firm young body whilst her travelling companion, lithe Margaret Drake of the shapely hooter and soulful brown eyes, tries to prevent intercourse breaking out – but hist, what ist? As I try and restrain Elisabeth's importunate (another class word, folks. Treasure it) fingers, two more mits slide round my waist and make instant contact with my zipper. My trained detective's mind tells me that this can mean only one of three things: either Elisabeth has arms growing out of her kneecaps that I have not noticed before, or, a third party has entered the cabin, or – and this is the alternative I favour – Margaret has decided to find out whether there is any action to take a slice of. I must say I am a bit surprised, but then my modest nature always tends to underestimate the effect I have on women. They try and bottle it up, poor creatures, but there is no gainsaying rampant desire and eventually it has to break over me like a tidal wave. I sometimes wish that they could let it out more gradually so that there was less danger of them doing themselves a mischief but it is no good trying to change nature – I mean, look at the flies. No amount of DDT shifts them, does it? Perhaps my mistake was to believe that by camping it up I could succeed in damping down my magnetism. It is asking a bit much, isn't it? Also, I read in the paper that today's birds fancy blokes who look like Twiggy on a diet. In my present tempting guise I must be playing right into the hands of those who stand at the threshold of sexual equality and will brook no denial.

Certainly it is going to be difficult to persuade these Lea-crazed bints that I am a poufdah when Percy has come out of the traps like the winner of the 8.15 at Harringay. Best to let them get on with it and bring a few rays of sunshine into their deprived lives. It is easy to read their background, isn't it? Probably librarians in the non-fiction department of some turgid watering place where the last scandal involved the vicar finding some surplus on a choir boy's surplice. I bet they have saved up for years for this. Their first smoke, their first drop of the hard stuff. I just hope they don't feel too bad in the morning when they wake up and remember the unspeakable depravity they have indulged in. If only I could explain to them that I have this effect on nearly all women, then it probably would not come so hard to them. Something else that could well be coming hard to them is the old amber mamba which makes a harpoon gun seem like a bunch of 'forget-me-nots' in its present condition.

Margaret whips her hands up and down it a few times as if checking that it is in good working order and then starts fumbling with my belt. No sooner have her digits left the area than Elisabeth's move in and begin to harvest my nuts as Margaret tugs down my trousers and fleas and ants. Of course, I am not whistling through my teeth all this time but enlivening Liz's cakehole with the dazzling repertoire of kisses that have made my lips famous throughout South West London. The wicked little creature is writhing against the mattress like a piece of plaited elastic unwinding itself and the fact that she is wearing nothing beneath her dress is soon revealed to me. It just shows what lurks beneath the surface of these shy young girls once they start getting the rocks out of their knickers. And, talking of knickers, this bird isn't wearing any of those, either. I find this out when she hauls her dress up to her navel. Margaret has been no more than a rustle of clothing for the past few minutes and when she next drifts into my vision she is down to her nail varnish and signet ring.

'Come onsh, darlingsh,' she purrs. 'Slesh get you shrtipped for action.' She is talking to Elisabeth and nudges me aside so that she can help the bird's dress over her nut. I use this natural break to sort out my own over-clothed condition and in less time than it takes to inscribe the immortal name of Roger Carpenter we are all down to the flesh tints.

It is clear that dirty deeds are but seconds away and I leap forward nimbly to give my public their money's worth or – perhaps, more aptly – my pubics their honey's worth. I toy with the idea of the flying love dive and then decide against it. Flashy, but dangerous to both parties and liable to dislodge a life jacket. Better to romance her with a few sub hooter hits or misses and then taxi down to the plus feature prior to the slaughter of the dilly pot with the full frontal funny gun. Percy could pierce armoured plate in his current highly nubile condition and I am glad that I decided to be magnanimous – and still the class lingo flows from his pen – and give these birds a taste of ecstasy before it goes out of fashion. I plant my bottle on the side of the bed and usher Elisabeth into my arms. She is really quite a cute little bird. Nothing to shout 'Timber!' about in the knocker department but much better put together than anything you could knock up with your Meccano set.

I brush my lips backwards and forwards across her kiss feature – you can do it forwards and backwards without suffering permanent damage – and then blow gently on her eyelids. It must be magic, mustn't it? Elisabeth clearly thinks so because she digs her fingernails into my arms and sighs ecstatically.

'Oooh, that's lovely!' she breathes. 'Clever Maggy!'

'Hang on a minute!' I say. I mean, I am the one dishing out the goodies at this love fest, aren't I? How come Maggy suddenly starts getting a credit? I look down and – blimey! There is Margaret's bonce bouncing up and down on the feature I had such big plans for. Not only that but her brewer's bung is whizzing in and out like the dicky bird on a Swiss clock stuck at twelve o'clock.

'Oh Maggy!'

'Elisabeth!'

Elisabeth lets go of my arms and starts massaging Margaret's barnet and I am practically pushed off the bed. 'Look, madam, do you mind!' I say, making no attempt to keep the peeved note out of my James Joyce. There is no answer, possibly because the two birds are now necking and fiddling with each other's fundaments. This is disgusting! What do they think they are doing? They have usurped my prerogative and that can be very painful.

'Break it up, girls!' There is a note of pleading in my voice that goes unheeded. 'Girls?' They don't seem to care about me any more. I might as well not be here. I try and massage Margaret's sit feature but she pushes my hand away. The depraved creature has clearly used me as a means of furthering her base designs.

'Elisabeth,' I say. 'Miss Uttley. Remember how you felt about me? Couldn't you feel that way again?' But Miss Uttley does not seem to be in the mood for conversation. She and her chum are winding up to a slow motion grumble mumble. It makes me want to cry just to look at them. What is the matter with me? Why have I been discarded in the full flower of my youth?

'Can't I play?' I say.

'That's beautiful!' breathes Elisabeth. 'Oh darling Maggy. I've never felt like this!'

'I told you,' husks Miss Drake. 'Ooooouuuuuuuuurrr-rggghhh!'

'I can do that,' I say. 'Look, let me have a go.'

But they don't look. 'Go away!' says Elisabeth showing all the gratitude experience will teach you to expect from a woman.

Dogged to the bitten end, I decide to have one more go. 'There must be something I can do to bring you satisfaction,' I say.

Elisabeth raises her head and brushes the hair from her thighs.

'All right,' she says. 'Bring me the vibrator.'

'The vibrator!' I say.

'It's at the bottom of the black suitcase, next to the hair drier.'

'You don't want a vibrator!' I say. 'You've got the real thing here. No batteries, no mains electricity, no attachments—'

'No erection,' says Elisabeth. I look down and she is right.

Always swift to catch the drift, Percy has packed it in and is representing less threat than Wee Georgie Wood in an Olympic High Jump Final. I don't usually like to admit defeat but this evening I think there is only one thing for it – point Percy at the door and walk after him fast.

CHAPTER EIGHT

In which Timmy helps out at the Rankins' cocktail party and attempts to calm an American lady who has had a drop too much.

'It's funny,' I say. 'But I don't feel like a sailor.'

'There's nothing funny about that,' says Sid. 'I don't feel like a sailor, either. Come to that, I don't fancy anything at the moment. I don't think I've recovered from Muna's farewell party.'

It is several days after my depressing evening with Misses Uttley and Drake, and Muna has gone ashore at Algiers. Apparently she has relations at Tizi Ouzou – though I would not be surprised if she had relations anywhere. Very hot-blooded she is.

'I didn't mean that, Sid,' I say. 'I was referring to the fact that we never get up to anything nautical. We could be working in a fall-out shelter but for the recurrent bouts of sea-sickness. When I came on this little jaunt I thought I was going to be standing against the masthead with spume breaking all over my face.'

'What a disgusting imagination you have,' says Sid. 'You're as bad as the rest of them.'

'Oh Sid,' I say. 'You must know what I mean. Haven't you ever tried a Hornblower?'

Sid's face turns scarlet. 'Now you've gone too far,' he says. 'Those cosmetics have gone to your head.'

'I meant Captain Hornblower.'

'They have grades for it, do they?' says Sid. 'That's really disgusting. You've quite put me off my cornflakes.'

'Captain Hornblower, RN,' I explain patiently. 'They're books by some geezer called C. S. Forester. All about the British Navy thumping the guts out of the frogs and assorted wog nations. Hornblower works his way through the ranks.'

'I'm not surprised to hear it,' says Sid. 'He doesn't sound the kind of bloke you'd like to find pissing beside you. I'm surprised your mum let you read stuff like that.'

'Surely you must have read some seafaring books when you were a kid?' I say. 'What about Coral Island.'

'Never heard of her,' says Sid. 'Anyway, what's a bird going to know about being a sailor? It's ridiculous.'

After that, I give it up. It is impossible to have an intelligent discussion with Sid about the arts. He is not interested in anything higher than a pair of top bollocks.

My only contact with the ship's crew is two of the blokes I am supposed to look after, the ship's doctor, Lieutenant Macpherson, and Sub-Lieutenant Rathbone. Macpherson looks like a badger during the moulting season but he is a definite favourite with the middle-aged to elderly old birds who line up outside his cabin for a handful of sleeping pills and the reassuring pressure of his stethoscope. There are quite a lot of widows on the look-out for a spot of companionship in their later years and they all seem to fancy the doc. I don't know quite what it is. I suppose he is a professional man and approachable – and they reckon that he must have seen much worse in his time. Macpherson seems much more interested in what he describes as 'a wee drappie', and though he has a photograph of a woman and five kids prominently displayed on his desk, I don't reckon he is married. When I am tidying up, I find three more 'wife and kids' photographs in the drawer with the four empty brandy bottles and the hip flask. I reckon he allows himself a change of photograph every voyage. Of course, he could be a bigamist, but from the way he talks about women – 'the monstrous regiment' is what he calls them – I don't think it is likely.

Young Rathbone is a real pain up the elephant and nothing I do for him is ever right. I suppose it is because every other officer on the ship treats him like a Richard the Third and he has to get his own back on someone. He grumbles about everything from his early morning tea to the way I hang up his uniform and I would cheerfully walk out on him if it didn't mean swimming a couple of hundred miles to thumb a lift home .What also gets up my bracket is the way that all the class frippet on the boat has the hóts for him. He is no older than me and if you took away the uniform there would be very little left. Birds are always slipping notes under his cabin door suggesting that they get together for a drink and when the posh nobs give a party they always invite Nicholas along. He is like a blooming debs' delight. You would think he would be grateful, too, but not a bit of it.

'Oh, not tedious Mrs Thomson,' he will say, his upper lip curling back against the end of his hooter. 'I couldn't stomach another evening in her company. And that terrible girl making calf's eyes at me. I think I'll send you along, Lea. It's about your mark.' I could cheerfully do a bit of landscape gardening on his mug but it is not until I catch a whiff of a familiar fragrance in his cabin that I start getting really worried. Is my Irish rose deceiving me or can I detect the haunting pong of the beautiful Caroline Rankin? Surely she cannot be wasting herself on this overgrown sea cadet? To add to my consternation, Rathbone is humming a merry melody to himself as he slaps after-shave lotion on to his unappealing boat race. It is not a pleasant sight.

'Tripping the light fantastic, are we?' I say.

Rathbone winces. 'How many times do I have to tell you? You call me Sir. What I do is my own affair.' He smiles to himself as if at a private joke.

'Another of those boring drinks parties, is it, sir?'

Rathbone gazes at himself in the mirror and takes a deep appreciative breath. You can see that it was love at first sight. 'This one isn't so boring,' he says. 'Have you seen that Rankin girl? Splendid looking creature.'

'Caroline Rankin?' I say, my pulse quickening.

'Good heavens. How did you know that? You chaps have your noses in everything, don't you?' Rathbone pulls his bow tie tight and taps the knot. 'Ah well, toodle pip. Don't wait up for me.'

'Only with a shot gun,' I breathe to myself.

Love's young nightmare waltzes off and I am retiring thoughtfully to my humble quarters when I bump into Pervis.

'Ah, Lea,' he says. 'Don't run away. I've got a job for you. Cook is catering for a private party and he needs another waiter. Get round to the galley.'

'Marvellous,' I say. 'I knew I'd end up as a galley slave if I hung around here long enough.'

'They also wait who only stand and serve,' sneers Pervis. 'Let's see if you can satisfy appetites when they present themselves in a vertical position.'

I am still trying to work out what he means when I report to the Becher's Brook. 'Right,' he says, rubbing the sweat off his face with a paper serviette which he then lays over a plate of cucumber sandwiches. 'I want you to circulate with the canapes.'

'Couldn't I turn lazy circles with the sausage rolls?' I ask him.

'Don't take the piss, you know what a canape is?'

'Yeh. It's one of those things that goes over the lifeboats.'

'That's a canopy, son. Don't push your luck with me. A canape is one of these tempting little savoury snacks that the nobs like to pass round while they're getting smashed. Take a couple of plates round to two four eight and don't eat them yourself. Also, don't clean your nails with the sausage sticks – especially when they've still got the sausages on them. Put that white jacket on and don't reach across the birds – in fact, don't be sick over anybody.'

I am not overthrilled about going back to my time as a waiter but it will provide a change of scene and get me away from Fatima for a bit – I have not told you about her yet, have I? Better wait till I have got this chapter off my chest.

It is a bit choppy going through the Sicilian Channel and one sausage rolls half the length of the companionway before I catch up with it. I should have left it really because it picks up more fluff than a boiled sweet in a toddler's pocket. The meringues don't stand up so well either and by the time I have got most of the black marks off they look as if someone has played cricket with them. Still, nobody can say that I am not trying to do a good job. Finding two four eight is no problem because the sound of upper class rabbit can be heard cabins away.

'How many knots do you think we've made today, Tony?' 'Henriettta won a bottle of sherry in the sweep. Ghastly sweet muck.' 'Were you at Dartmouth or Pangbourne, Nicholas?'

The last remark pulls me up with a start. It was dumb of me but I had not associated Rathbone and the Rankin knees up with my detail. Feeling my heart start to thump, I probe the cluster of guzzling bodies for – ah, there she is. Looking like one of those birds Prince Charles is always supposed to be about to marry. I bet she looks smashing in a headscarf. Some old geezer with acres of gold bands round his sleeves is clearly boring the fleas and ants off her but that beautiful penny a mile remains glued to her boat race.

'Eeerw!' The noise is made by Mrs Rankin when she sees me standing in the doorway and is accompanied by an expression of worried distaste. I can sense that she would like to say 'Not today, thank you' and slam the door in my mug. I must take immediate steps to make a good impression. She may be an old ratbag but, who knows, she could end up as my mum-in-law.

'Good evening, Mrs Rankin,' I say, stepping forward briskly and shoving my tray of goodies under her hooter. 'Would you care for a merringoo?'

'Er . . .' Mrs Rankin looks round anxiously and without taking her mince pies off me, stretches out a nervous hand. It is only as it closes round a meringue that I notice she has selected one which has copped a piece of sausage as an addition to the cream.

'No!' I say, shooting out a hand just as she gets the meringue to her cakehole. 'Not that—' I suppose I do grab it a bit hard really but, even so, I am surprised at the way the cream squirts down the inside of Mrs Rankin's dress. 'Oh dear,' I say. 'I am sorry.' There is nowhere to prop the tray so I shove it into the hands of the old geezer with the gold circles round his sleeves and scrape my sticky mit against the side of it. 'Excuse me,' I say. 'I'm just going to get the sausage out.' I can just see it sliding down between Mrs Rankin's powerful knockers so I pull back my sleeve and gingerly insert my mit.

'What the devil?' Trust Rankin to shove his hooter in at a moment like this. 'Get away from my wife!' Before I can explain about the sausage, Rankin grabs me by the arm and yanks me away from his old lady. Unfortunately, the brass button on my cuff gets caught in the row of loops along the front of Mrs Rankin's dress and before anyone can shout 'take cover!' there is a loud ripping noise and Mrs Rankin's breastworks are revealed.

'You – you—!' For a moment, I think that Rankin is going to belt me one. While his old lady screams and runs out of the room, he turns an ugly shade of pink and quivers like a guardsman having a joddrell in a sentry box.

'What is happening here?' The nautical geezer shoves the tray back in my hands and helps himself to a sausage.

'I'm sorry, Captain,' splutters Rankin. 'This – this—'

It occurs to me that this is probably a good moment to move on, so I burrow into the mass of bodies, most of whom missed out on the sausage incident. I am not very happy to find the Captain down here because I am wondering who can be driving the ship. It may have an automatic pilot but can that detect icebergs? I know that these are fairly infrequent in the Mediterranean but I have never been a man to take chances. I think that the Captain should finish his gin and get back to the bridge, pronto.

'Were you responsible for that fracas, Lea?' The voice belongs to rat-features Rathbone who is irritably tapping the side of his glass like a woodpecker trying to get into a lamp-post. The fair Caroline has moved to his side. She nods at me with what I intercept as a gesture of muted passion.

'No, sir.' I am not certain what a fracas is so I don't reckon that I am lying. 'Would you care for one of these?'

'What are they?' says Rathbone. It always gets up my bracket the way people say that when you shove a tray of perfectly obvious sausages and meringues under their hoot-ters. I mean, they are a bit bashed about but nobody could mistake them for ratchet screwdrivers.

'I'll have a sausage,' says Caroline. She raises one to her lips and nibbles its end in a way that makes a tingle run down my tonk. 'Oh scrumptious!' she says. 'Do try one, Nick. I love them when they're a bit burnt.'

'There's another one down here somewhere,' I say, always eager to please. 'Hang on a moment and I'll sort it out for you.'

'Don't touch them with your filthy hands!' scolds Rathbone.

'Don't be insensitive,' says Caroline. 'He was only trying to be helpful.'

'That's right,' I say. 'Anyway, they don't walk on to these sticks, you know. If you just try and prick them they drop on the floor. Some digital pressure is necessary.'

Rathbone starts to bristle. 'Listen!' he says. 'I'm not interested in discussing how sausages get on sticks with you. Go about your business or I'll report you to Mr Pervis.'

'Fancy another one before I go?' I say, turning to Caroline. 'Take two if you like. And why not stock up with a merringoo while you're about it? There's certain to be a rush on them later. That's a good one – next to the one with the fag ash on it.'

'You heard what I said, Lea!' hisses Rathbone. 'Remember your place.'

'We don't have any plaice,' I say. 'Just those sardines on little pieces of toast. Frankly, I reckon they're a bit soggy myself, but you may—' At this point an expression comes over Rathbone's face like the one I saw on Charles Laughton's mug just before he had Clark Gable dragged under the *Bounty* a few times like he was trying to polish the hull with him. It is not a pleasant sight and I hug my sausages to me and move on. I will return to spellbind Caroline when nit-features has pissed off.

'What you got on that tray, fella?' The bird addressing me could only be a ham shank. She is wearing enough make-up to kit out a kiddy's paintbox and the kind of dress that went out of fashion when Rita Hayworth stopped having bridesmaids. She is leaning against a bulkhead like she needs the support and her glass is tilted dangerously near to pouring over the floor.

'Sausages and meringoos, madam,' I say.

'What you limeys call bangers, huh?' she says. She emphasises 'banger' like the word appeals to her.

'That's right,' I say. 'Hot dogs without the bun and the mustard.'

'No mustard.' Her drink sways dangerously and I steady it. 'I'm stoned,' she says. This cannot be news to anyone and I wonder what to say. 'You don't have anything on that tray that appeals to me. I hate the sight of those little sausages. Give me a frankfurter every time!' The lady does not have a voice that would easily turn on a turtle dove and I turn the tray round and shove the meringues at her. 'Aw Gard! They're disgusting!'

'It's the hot lights,' I say. 'They don't usually fall apart like that.'

Mrs America takes a deep drag at her fag and expels the smoke through her hooter so that it disappears down her cleavage. 'A real bunch of stuffed shirts' she says nodding around the company. 'None of them will look you in the eyes.' Not surprising, I think to myself. I mean, her mince pies are all right but it is her bristols that command attention – especially if you were an engineer or designed railway buffers.

'They look as if they're ashamed to be alive. They haven't got an ounce of spunk in their whole bodies.' I am not certain whether this last statement is altogether surprising. I mean, I don't know what kind of stocks one carries but it can't be a lot more than an ounce, can it?

'You look as if you need a drink.'

'I couldn't have one here,' I say.

'Nobody's going to mind.' She lifts her glass to my lips and I turn my head aside. 'No, I couldn't. I'd be in dead schtuck if I did. There's too many people watching.'

'Come neshxt door. There's nobody there. I'll bring you one.'

Of course, I should say definitely not and proceed upon my business but I am curious because I have a feeling that the lady is interested in more than stopping me from getting thirsty. The feeling starts six inches above my right knee where my cobblers are being caressed by a hand which is not attached to either of my arms. This could be the start of something big and one part of my body that clearly agrees with the sentiment is my Mad Mick. I look round nervously. The last thing I want is any more unpleasantness and maybe it would be a good idea to get this transatlantic tonk tweaker somewhere where she can stretch out on a bed and sleep it off.

'Hang on a minute – not to that!' I brush aside her marauding mit and stick my head round the door that connects with one of the bedrooms of the Rankin apartment. 'Sorry!' I shut the door quickly. What a pity that Mrs Rankin was in the middle of putting on a new dress. I hope she won't get the idea that – oh well, it's no good worrying about that now.

'I like you. You're a ballsy guy!' Mrs America is certainly in a position to have proved that statement correct and I take more evasive action and apologise to the old bird who gets meringue all over her shoulder.

'Would you like the rest of it?' I say. 'They're very – eek!' I break off when my American friend gives me another playful poke in the nut field.

'Stash the hash and let's find a quiet corner,' she husks. 'I like the cut of your jib, sailor.'

I take another quick butchers round the room and see that Caroline is still trying to pretend that she is interested in whatever tedious drivel Rathbone is feeding into her earhole and that old man Rankin is giving the Captain a verbal blow job. With a bit of luck, I will be able to tuck Mrs America away without anyone noticing. I open another door and find a bedroom that is empty except for all the things that would tell you that it was a bedroom in the first place.

'In here,' I whisper. I look round but there is no sign of my new friend. 'I'm standing behind you,' she says.

You can't fault the Yanks when it comes to action, can you? How she moves so fast and still keeps a glass in her hand is a mystery to me. 'Would you like to put your feet up?' I say.

'Do I look like a contortionist?'

'I meant would you like to lie down? You might feel better.'

'I feel great.' Mrs America digs her fingernails into my forearm. 'It's you I'm worried about. You haven't had your drink yet.' She shoves her glass towards my lips and I take a nervous sip. By the cringe! Lipstick-flavoured gin with the merest touch of paint stripper to give it body. No wonder the lady is swaying from side to side. Or is it just the booze? I can't see anything out of the porthole but the vessel is definitely pitching and tossing. Stand by, folks. We could be in for a bumpy ride.

'Good, huh?'

'I prefer a beer, actually,' I say.

'What the hell, it's all booze.' She knocks back the contents of her glass. 'My name's Mame.'

'Do you spell that M-A-I-M?' I ask as her right hand makes another vicious descent on my action man kit.

'I like you,' she says. 'Put it there.' Normally, when people say that, you expect to shake hands with them but Mame is different. She means 'put it there'. And if you have any difficulty working out where 'there' is, she pulls up her dress and puts your hand on it. This is madness. I should be back in the state room working the old mind-boggling chat on Caroline, not trying to save my zipper from the big dipper.

'I must leave you now,' I say.

'Leave me?' Mame lurches against me so that I am pressed back against the cabin door. Behind my left ear-hole, I can hear music. They must have started dancing. How very nice. 'What do you mean, leave me? You haven't even got near me yet.'

'But I'm supposed to be handing round the nosh next door,' I plead.

'Forget it. They don't need food, they need blood transfusions. Kiss me.' It is nice of Mame to give me the option but in fact her lips grind against mine like a couple of sticks of sealing wax dropped on a hot griddle. Down Percy! The sensation-hungry fool is playing right into her hands – and I mean hands. 'Come on, baby. Let's build a bridge between our two great countries.'

'We just did,' I grunt. 'Please! I must—' But what chance have I got? My trousers are round my ankles and you could hang the Spar Spangled Banner from my erect hampton. Mame clearly has other plans for it.

"'That's what I call a night stick,' she breathes. 'Don't go away, fella, you're just about to do your good deed for the day.' Surely there must be some means of escape? Before I can think of it, Mame makes another murderous assault on my lips and reveals that she has a crafty way of flicking her panties to one side, just as your Uncle Herbert might do if he was having a gypsy's kiss.

'OK hump me, Humphrey!' she hollers. 'Carry me back to old Virginny!' And with that she vaults on to my hampton like he was Champion the Wonder Horse.

It is most athletically done and for a largish woman you have to hand it to her – in fact you don't have to hand it to her, she comes and takes it for herself. Loth as I am to take on this additional burden I have to confess that there are many things I would much sooner not have jumping on my dick – Idy Amin's fan club to name but one of them. I up my mits around Mame's generous sit feature and stagger away from the door as the *Tern* pitches into a trough. We totter across the cabin and end up with her bottle stuck against the wash basin. This takes a lot of the weight off my mind and other places and I wang Percy in and out until all the toothbrushes jump out of the plastic beaker.

'That's my boy!' grunts Mame. 'Hump me, hump me!' I am doing the best I can and even beginning to enjoy it a little as the ship gives another lurch and we stagger back into the centre of the floor. Luckily, I have long since kicked off my round the houses and can concentrate on keeping my balance and trying to control the sack of serpents that is going ape against my bridge of sighs. Mame has her legs crossed behind my back and is clearly building up to what might be described as a grandstand finish. For a woman not in the first flower of youth she is certainly an athletic performer.

'Go on, baby!' she bellows. 'That's great!' I am trying to remember some of those old Carmen Miranda numbers but the strain is not so much on my memory as on my you-know-what. Every shake of the maraccas threatens my knackers. Mame is leaning back as far as she can go whilst still hanging on to my neck; her head is tilted and her long, tawny barnet hanging down towards the carpet. Right, lady! Here we-ooops! The ship gives another lurch and I totter back towards the door. Click. The noise is accompanied by an upsurge in the volume of music. Don't say that someone has opened the—

"WAAAAAARGH!" My shoulders are braced to meet the door but – they don't. Still firmly slotted into Mame I catch a glimpse of Rankin's astonished face and find myself travelling backwards through a bewildered crowd of dancers. The unforgettable strain of Victor Sylvester playing 'You're The Cream In My Coffee' brushes against my lughole and I am through another door, colliding with the wall of the corridor. Over Mame's shoulder I can see Mrs Rankin staring at me open-mouthed.

'I'll be back for the tray later,' I say reassuringly. Mrs Rankin starts to buckle at the knees and is supported by a couple of her guests. I know how she feels.

'Don't stop!' urges Mame. 'I think I'm going to come again.'

CHAPTER NINE

In which Timmy and Sid experience the delights of Fatima, a belly dancer inexorably wedded to her craft.

'What's this I hear about you giving dancing lessons?' says Sid.

I lie back on my bunk and close my eyes. 'Do me a favour, Sid,' I groan.

'I suppose it was your success at the Palais. Went straight to your little dancing feet. I might have guessed as much. Trying to emulate Fred Astaire, were you?'

'Don't be filthy,' I say. 'I've never even seen the bloke.' That's the trouble with life aboard a boat. Rumours fly around like wild flowers – or is it wildfire? It doesn't matter. Either way, if you pissed down the inside of your trouserleg everybody would know about it before you had pulled up your zipper.

'Of course, it could have been Fatima,' says Sid. 'You've been surrounded by stimuli lately, haven't you? I do wish she wouldn't leave her yashmaks all over the cabin, there's nowhere to hang my socks.'

'I wouldn't mind if you washed them first,' I groan. 'Just hanging them up doesn't do any good.'

'It lets the air through them,' says Sid.

'That's not air,' I say. 'By the time it gets here it's been used by everyone else in the ship.'

'It's ridiculous three people living in this space,' grumbles Sid. 'I said that when Muna was here. Look! She's left her smalls in the basin.'

'What, Muna?'

'No, Fatima. They're just like ours, aren't they?'

'They may be just like yours, but they're not just like mine,' I say.

'Don't be daft. I meant just like Western ones. It takes the glamour away from it somehow.'

'I wish someone would take Fatima away,' I say. 'I don't know how we got lumbered with her.'

'What a load of cobblers!' says Sid. 'It was your idea in the first place. I was quite happy to leave her with the Arab geezer. Especially when he explained how his little hooked knife worked.'

'I don't remember that,' I say.

'Of course you don't,' says Sid. 'You were Chopin before we even got to the Casbah. Don't you remember how you wanted to buy a camel saddle for your mum?'

'Oh yeh,' I say. 'Then we found out that the bloke had sold me the camel as well.'

'Not just one of them,' says Sid. 'I remember what a berk you looked with them all straggling behind you as you went into the night club.'

'I don't remember that, either,' I say.

'I'm not surprised,' says Sid. 'Your memory has a habit of clouding over when it gets to the embarrassing bits.'

'Embarrassing, Sid?'

'I think you could describe it as that,' says Sid. 'Nobody particularly minded when the big smelly one ate the accordion, but when the small smelly one relieved itself over the piano there were a few cries of "bad show!" in Arabic – and not just from the bloke who was playing it at the time.'

'Oh yes, Sid!' I say. 'It's beginning to come back. There was some unpleasantness with Fatima's partner, wasn't there?'

'She seemed to think it was unpleasant, Timmo. From what I can remember, the camel rather liked it. So did the customers. Only the manager was worried that they'd take his licence away. Apparently, it's not considered a tourist attraction any more.'

'I remember that,' I say. 'But what I can't remember is how we met Fatima.'

'It was during the dance of the seven veils,' says Sid.

'She was dancing it, was she?'

'No, Timmo, *you were*. She was one of the people trying to drag you off the floor. Mind you, I don't blame her. I thought you were going it a bit when you started singing I've got a lovely bunch of coconuts.'

'They probably didn't understand, Sid.'

'I think they did, Timmy. You were waving them at the audience at the time.'

'Sid! That's terrible. Why didn't you stop me?'

'I was too busy trying to get the camels out of the ladies' toilet.'

'Blimey! We won't be able to go back there again.'

'Nobody will, Timmo. Surely you remember the fire?'

'I didn't start that, did I?'

'Not directly, Timmo. The fire-eater got hiccups. It was very nasty. He was going off like a roman candle. When we got him to a window he had half the street alight in three hiccups.'

'How terrible, Sid. Was anyone hurt?'

'A few people got brushed against the walls when the camels climbed on to the fire engine.'

'Why did they want to do that, Sid?'

'It was blocking the road they were stampeding down. You know how narrow the streets are. More like alleys, really. I remember how frustrated the firemen were. They connected up to the nearest hydrant and sprayed everybody with cockroaches.'

'Where was I, Sid?'

'You were still in the gent's with Fatima. Very brave of you, I must say. None of the camels would go in there. I'm surprised you can't remember it. You appeared to have formed a very deep attachment for each other – well, about six inches, anyway.'

'Oh yeh. She was showing me how to do a belly dance.'

'Ah. So that's why the shithouse fell down. I thought it wasn't just faulty corrugated iron.'

'Yes! It's all coming back to me. The manager kept asking her to go back to his place after the show and she wasn't that kind of girl.'

'That's what you told me, Timmo.'

'He said that if she didn't play ball with him, she'd lose her spot.'

'That's right. Mind you, I think she should have been grateful to lose any of her spots. Still, love is blind, I suppose. Especially when you're stoned out of your tiny mind. Anyhow, what's a few blackheads when you've got a complexion like that?'

'I can't remember how we got on the boat, Sid.'

'You wouldn't, would you? You'd fallen asleep between her knockers leaving it for me to work out. Why you had to mention we were going to Malta I'll never know. It was a certainty she had some bleeding relation there.'

'How did we get aboard, Sid?'

'We borrowed the fire engine, didn't we? I do wish you had waited until I undid some of those hoses. That poor devil at the top of the ladder must have got the shock of his life when he fell into the Sultan's harem – especially as the old bugger was ninety-two. Some of those birds hadn't tasted flesh for fifteen years. I believe they had difficulty identifying his helmet.'

'Was I driving, Sid?'

'Yeh. You suddenly woke up, grabbed the wheel and shouted "Me Ben Hur!" Then we were off. You reversed so fast that most of the camels fell off before we got to the first bend. Then it was straight down to the waterfront with the hoses trailing behind us like we were leaving a wedding reception.'

'Blimey. I must have been pissed.'

'You were, Timmo. Otherwise you would never have tried to drive straight out to the ship. I remember thinking you were going it a bit when you went down the jetty at eighty.'

'Gawd strewth! How did I stop?'

'I don't know. I got off soon after we hit the water. It's a blooming good job camels are powerful swimmers, that's all I can say.'

'Probably why they call them the ships of the desert, Sid. Is that how we got back to the *Tern*. On a camel?'

'That's right, Timmo. Fatima, you, me and Nigel.'

'Nigel?'

'That's the camel. I think Fatima's feeding him at the moment.'

'We've got a camel down here, Sid! What about the smell?'

'He's getting used to it. Mind you, he didn't care for it much at first but once I moved him into the first class baggage hold he's settled down a treat. He's eaten three trunks already.'

Whilst I lie back and consider the amazing – and disturbing – lapses of memory that have prevented me from recapturing the full flavour of these incidents, Fatima returns with the news that we will have to change Nigel's name.

'Allah be praised, cor blimey,' she says – I think she was the result of a mixed marriage; I mean, mixed in more senses than that her father was a man and her mother a woman or vice versa – 'The camel has calved already.'

'Strewth,' says Sid. 'That accounts for all those trunks. She was eating for two.'

'Or making a nest,' I say – I was always interested in nature when I was a kid.

'Camels aren't like that,' says Sid. 'They're very unsentimental animals. With them it's just a question of bang! and there you are: a sprog camel. Very few people get close to camels – except, of course, Fatima's friend at the El Toupee.'

'Is very sweet, the noo,' sighs Fatima. 'It makes me feel bloudy.'

'What do you mean, darling?' says Sid. 'Bloody or broody?'

It is not a question I have to ask. When I look into those melting brown eyes, it all comes back to me. The stars peeping over the corrugated iron walls of the khazi, the subdued rustle of a million flies, Fatima spilling out of my arms. Memories are made of moments like that.

'I think I dance, stone the crows.' Fatima squeezes both her hands into fists and shuts her eyes in concentration.

'Do us a favour, darling,' says Sid. 'Not now. There isn't room.' But Fatima's belly has already started its slow warm-up – like a cement mixer on a cold morning. That brings back memories too. As the first ripple passes through her pelvis my September morn turns to toffee. Sid's back presses against the wall beside mine and Fatima starts snapping her fingers and brings down two pairs of Sid's socks.

'Fry's Turkish Delight,' she warbles. 'Let's have it off toni-i-i-ght!'

'They don't write them like that any more,' says Sid. 'Very nice, darling. Don't ring us, we'll ring you.'

But Fatima is clearly under the influence of her calling and chucking her tummy about like she is trying to get rid of it. You cannot help noticing because she only wears this belt round the hips with tassles hanging from it and a bra that sprouts long bits of string from the part where you would look for her strawberries if you were trying to impress your biology master.

'Mind what you're doing with those knockers,' says Sid. 'I don't mind having a whip round but this is ridiculous.'

'Sorry, cobber,' says Fatima. 'I take it off.'

'I didn't mean that!' says Sid. 'Don't—' But the deadly bristol harness has already been shed and the rampant knockers allowed to run riot. 'Duck, you fool!' shouts Sid.

'What's the point?' I say. 'If she misses you with the Manchesters you walk straight into her Derby Kell.'

'We've got bloody Nigel to blame for this!' snarls Sid. 'Just as I thought she'd cooled down, too. Get off me!' He is addressing Fatima's belly which is grinding against his giggle stick like you are glad it does not have a circle of sandpaper attached to it.

'Sidney like, not 'arf?' she says.

Sidney is hardly in a position to argue with her if 'like' means having an attack of the instant bananas. Fatima starts bending her knees and perking up and down, and beads of sweat break out on Sid's forehead.

'Fatima, please stop that,' he says. 'Sidney got to go help organise draw for ship's log.'

'It look like the ship's log down the front of Sid's trousers,' I say, always ready with a playful word in adversity.

I am soon sorry that I opened my big trap. 'Timmy like dance with me, jig jig?' she says, reaching behind her in a gesture which I am certain does not mean that she is about to scratch a mosquito bite. I do not think that she is referring to an Irish jig and this supposition is proved correct when her tassels land on top of Sid's socks and we cop a view of nether fuzz that looks like an aerial photograph of Epping Forest.

'Blimey!' says Sid. 'I always wondered what they wore under their kilts.'

No further comment is immediately possible because Fatima lays hands upon our zippers and whips them down like she is trying to keep pace with Britain's standard of living.

'Fry's Turkish Delight,' she croons. 'That looks a bit of orl right!' She is clearly referring to the hampton parking lot that has been revealed by her immodest gesture and which she is touching up like an enthusiastic gardener checking that her young marrows have not been nipped by an early frost. Satisfied that everything in the vegetable plot is up to scratch, she gives us another buffeting with her belly button – she can put it into reverse so fast that you would swear she had two of them – and indicates by the subtle pressure of her mits on our shoulders – it is like a telegraph pole falling on you – that we should sink to the floor.

'Now,' she says. 'I dive bomb you with the love hutch, cor blimey!'

'Thank God, Hitler didn't have her during the Blitz,' says Sid.

I do not reply because I am busy weighing up the whirling grumble that is circling above me. It is like half a ton of jelly babies mated with jumping beans. Pathetically unprepared for what is to come – in the sense of arrival rather than despatch – my Marquis of Lorne stands up proudly smack in the flight path of the deadly dilly pot. It nods a couple of times as the first vibrations hit and then – 'THWOP!!' Fatima swoops out of the sun and it has disappeared. For a terrible moment, I think she has shaved it clean off and then I catch a glimpse of its silvery shaft as Fatima jerks her tum into reverse and the honey combs start melting against the walls of my hive.

'How do you like 'em?' says Sid. 'Boiled or scrambled?'

CHAPTER TEN

In which Timmy achieves a date with Caroline and attempts to unload a couple of camels.

'Well, that's her gone,' says Sid. 'Now we've only got to sort out the camel.'

'Camels,' I say.

We are watching Fatima willow down the gangway as the *Tern* lies at anchor in the Grand Harbour, Valletta, Malta. It is an impressive sight. Huge, seemingly unconnected structures looming out at all angles – the harbour is pretty striking, too.

'The George Cross Island,' I say.

'They should be in line for another one if they can withstand her for a couple of weeks,' says Sid. 'Look out, she's waving!' We duck down behind a lifeboat. 'We don't want an action replay of that scene with Muna. You remember how emotional she got when she wanted to change her mind about staying with her aunty and we had to take a firm line?'

'I still don't think you should have sold her to that bloke,' I say.

'What are you on about! She was only going to be a receptionist. She wasn't going to have to do anything untoward. I'd have trusted my own wife with that geezer.'

'Yeh, but Rosie's different. She's more experienced, isn't she?'

It occurs to me as I speak that mentioning my sister in these terms is not going to go over big with Sid and I am right.

'What do you mean?' he says. 'What are you trying to imply? Are you looking for a punch up the throat?' It is funny how the blokes who are always on the look-out for a Friar Tuck are the ones who do their nuts if you so much as suggest that their old lady is not a dead ringer for Snow White. I could tell Sid things about Rosie before they got spliced that would turn his barnet white as a polar bear's wet dream – but what is the point? She was just going through a stage that lots of young girls go through – even if she did go through it a few more times than most. Let him who is without sin throw up the first, as it says in the Bible.

'I'm sorry, Sid,' I say. 'I just meant that Rosie has an emotional maturity that stands her in good stead in this kind of situation. You could flog her to an Arab brothel keeper without experiencing any qualms.'

'Course I could,' says Sid. 'That's what I was trying to tell you. Don't keep contradicting me. You end up revealing your ignorance.'

'Sorry, Sid,' I say, deciding that the subject of Rosie's morals is one best put aside. 'What do you reckon we ought to do about Margaret and Harold?'

'I dunno,' says Sid. 'It's a piece of cake getting birds on and off the ship – provided they wear as much make-up as the crew – but camels are difficult. I remember the way the bloke looked at us when we came aboard at Algiers. If he hadn't been so wrapped up in watching the town burning, it could have been awkward.'

'We'll have to get them off soon,' I say. 'Harold has got his mother's appetite. I took a geezer who wanted to get something out of his trunk down to the hold and there was only the lock left.'

'The lock of the hold?' shrieks Sid.

'No, the trunk,' I say.

Sid looks relieved. 'You had me worried, there. I know what they're like. What did you tell the bloke?'

'I told him it was rats, Sid.'

'Good thinking, Timmo. Did he believe you?'

'I think his credulity was a bit stretched, Sid. He trod in one of Margaret's Richard the Thirds.'

'Cobblers! She is naughty, that camel. I've tried everything to house-train her but she doesn't want to know. Newspapers, little boxes of cinders. She eats the lot. This bloke didn't catch a glimpse of her, did he?'

'No, Sid. She and Harold were browsing down the other end of the hold. It's amazing how they can suck rivets out of the steel plates, isn't it?'

'Yes. I think they must have taught Fatima how to give a blow job. Anyway, none of this helps us get them off the boat, does it? I'm worried about Harold being brought up on a diet of cabin trunks. It can't be good for a young camel.'

'I reckon the only thing to do is to wait till this evening, Sid. Most of the passengers and crew will be ashore and there's a reception at Government House as well. With a bit of luck, we'll be the only people aboard.'

Sid's mince pies survey the dockside scene. 'Yeh. If we could borrow one of those cranes, we could winch them ashore, couldn't we? It can't be very difficult to use. I had something like that when I was a kiddy.'

I leave Sid making his master plan and skive off round the decks trying to look as if I am doing something vitally important to the efficient running of the ship. With a bit of practice you can spend a whole morning collecting three glasses. As is my wont, I dawdle round the outdoor swimming pool to check on the state of the knockers and am arrived just in time to clock the fair Caroline rising from the water like Afro-nightie – or whatever that Greek goddess of of love was called – and I don't mean Melina Murky. Her bathing costume fits closer than a french letter on a pillar box and when a couple of beads of water run down between her bristols you wonder how they find the room. I have not seen her since the night of her parents' party and I am a bit wary of how she is going to respond to me. I believe that Mrs Rankin has only just left the sickbay.

To my surprise, Caroline hauls herself out of the pool – it is a moving experience for Percy when she rests her knockers on the edge – and moves towards me with the grace of a young gazelle leaving the water hole. 'I've been wondering where you were,' she says. 'What on earth were you doing with that Mame woman? Daddy was absolutely furious.' She sounds eager and not a little impressed and it occurs to me that the earthy side of my nature may be what is most likely to score with this bird. In the past, I have often made the mistake of trying to toff myself up when I would have been better employed capitalising on my crude animal vigour.

'We became involved,' I say. My tone of voice is not exactly world weary but you get the impression that I become involved quite often.

'Gosh!' she says. 'It was so blatant.'

'Yeh,' I say. 'I'm sorry if you were shocked. Life's elemental forces can be a bit disturbing sometimes, can't they?'

Caroline looks even more impressed. 'I don't really know,' she says. 'I haven't come up against them very much. Daddy's awfully careful.'

'I should hope so,' I say. 'I mean—' I break off when I realise what she probably meant. 'Eer-yes. Still, you can't be careful all the time, can you? You can't legislate against these things.'

This 'legislate' word is a master stroke because it reveals a totally new dimension of my personality. It is also good for Scrabble. Bung a 'legis' before a 'late' or an 'islate' after a 'leg' and you are really cooking with gas – especially if you can land on a triple word score square. Anyway, I can see that Caroline is impressed with my grasp of the English language as well as my ability to hump ladies about on the end of my humpton – I mean, hampton – and that can't be bad.

'No,' she says. 'I suppose you can't. Perhaps I've led a very sheltered life but I just didn't believe things like that happened.'

'Things happen when people want them to,' I say, very Kojak. 'There's a lot of people on this boat looking for something.'

'I know,' says Caroline, brightly. 'It's the purser's treasure trail. Mummy wouldn't let me go in for it.'

I swallow a sigh. This kid is never going to be the new Barbara Stanwyck. 'What will your mother let you do?' I say, my lips puckering in a sardonic smile.

'She'll let me go to the reception at Government House with Sub-Lieutenant Rathbone,' says Caroline with spirit. My buoyant mood collapses like a ballooned prick. Rathbone! Just when I thought I was in for a romantic ramble round the ramparts and a moment of magic behind the Customs Shed. 'You won't be there, I suppose?'

She must be joking. 'I don't think it's very likely,' I say.

'What a shame,' she says. 'It sounds as if it's going to be super fun. The Americans are rolling up too.'

She points to an aircraft carrier that looks as if Sydney Opera House has drifted out to sea – which I believe some people have plans for it to do. 'They're here on a goodwill visit.'

'I heard about it,' I say. On shore, two bored looking geezers are trying to rub out the 'Yanks Go Home!' slogan painted on the sea wall.

'Cheer up,' she says. 'I'm certain you won't be lonely. Not if the other night was anything to go by.'

I cannot help feeling bitter, because it is quite clear that the bird fancies me and would much rather spend the evening in my scintillating company than with rat-features Rathbone.

How can fate be so unkind to he who should be her favourite son? Just because he was born on the wrong side of the tracks Cinders Lea does not cop an invitation to the palace knees-up. And where is my Buttons? Not even on the front of my fly now that I have changed to a zipper. The nearest I have got to a fairy godmother is Sid and if you gave him six rats to turn into white horses you would stand a good chance of ending up with thirty rats before you found a dollop of horse shit in front of your pumpkin.

It is, therefore, with heavy heart that I return to my labours and trudge round to Rathbone's cabin to change his bedclothes. I am not thrilled to find him there, nursing his nut between his mits and making groaning noises.

'Oh, it's you, Lea,' he says, sounding as if he shares my lack of enthusiasm for the encounter. 'I've got the devil of a headache. This perpetual junketing is getting me down.'

'Been making junkets have you, sir?' I say brightly. 'I never warmed to them much myself.'

'Don't play the fool with me!' snaps Rathbone. 'Leave that bed alone and go round to the quack and get me some aspirins.' He waves his hand towards the closet. 'Oh, and get my number one uniform pressed. I've got this thrash at Government House tonight.' His voice takes on a more cheerful note. 'I don't want to break Miss Rankin's heart, do I?'

I don't answer him but take his clobber and drop it off at my cabin on the way to Doctor Macpherson. It is quite a snappy uniform and I can't help thinking how much better it would look on me. No point in just thinking. I slip the jacket on – a bit tight under the arms, of course – and do up a few of the brass buttons. Uhm. Not bad. Not bad at all. I reckon I could break a few hearts in this lot. I try on the cap and – oh yes – devastating. A slight tilt to one side and it could be the young Cary Grant staring at me from the cracked mirror over the wash basin. I am just practising a few nautical expressions like 'Hat on your batches!' and 'Shorten your giblets!' when the door opens and I see Seaman Blout staring at me.

'Oh, sorry Sir,' he says. 'I didn't know – wait a minute! What do you think you're doing, Lea? It's a very serious offence impersonating an officer.'

'Don't get your knickers in a twist,' I say. 'I was just trying to see if it suited me.'

'Don't waste your time,' says Blout. 'You're never going to be wearing one outside your imagination.'

'Why don't you go and sprain your wrist?' I tell him. 'Don't you usually knock before you barge into people's cabins?'

'No need for that tone,' says Blout. 'I'm here on Mr Pervis's instructions. He was doing his rounds and he heard some strange braying noises.'

'That's Sid cleaning his teeth,' I say. 'I've complained to him about it but it hasn't done any good.'

'Sounds like an animal,' says Blout.

'Exactly,' I say. 'Very disturbing. I'll have another word with him about it.'

Blout has a few more words with me and coaxes his pectorals down the corridor leaving me thinking that the sooner we get shot of Margaret and Harold the better. Still one thing at a time. I had better nip round to Macpherson and get Rathbone's bleeding aspirins. I am approaching the good man's rory when, to my horror, it opens, and Mrs Mame emerges looking flushed about the area where her bushel joins her cabman's rest. Oh dear, this is the last thing I need at the moment – a Lea-crazed ham-shank wrenching my these and those off in broad daylight. I brace myself for the inevitable confrontation and am not a little surprised when the lady stares at me without a sign of recognition or interest and continues on her way down the corridor. That's nice, isn't it? After all we have meant to each other as well. With that gesture, she has sullied something beautiful.

I tap on the door and find Doctor Macpherson looking equally flustered. 'The shameless hussy!' he rasps. 'Revealing her braists before I'd so much as got the top off my fountain pen!'

'Is there anything the matter with her?' I say. I mean, you don't want to take any chances, do you.

'Galloping nymphomania at a guess,' growls Macpherson. 'Though I couldna' diagnose that to her face. Still—' he picks up a phial of tablets and waves it at me with an expression of grim satisfaction on his face, 'I think I've given her something else to keep her occupied for a few days.'

'Oh yes?' I say, hoping that he is going to tell me what, but not wanting to push it.

Macpherson spills a few tablets into the palm of his

hand and drops them on to the table. 'These'll loosen her bowels so she's no time for gallivanting. She won't be wandering far from her cabin once these wee pills have taken effect. Now, what can I do for you?'

Was it at that moment or when Macpherson turned to look for some aspirins that the great plan took shape in my mind? Perhaps it was staring at those little green pills that reminded me of the unhealthy tint of Rathbone's cheeks. With my rival's Enochs (Enoch Powells; Bowels. Ed.) in schtuck and his uniform in my possession – plus the fact that Seaman Blout has already mistaken me for an orificer – I must be in line for a crack at the title. At last fate's coming on strong with a bit of the nudge, nudge, wink, wink, in my direction.

Quick as a flasher, I scoop up some of the pills and have them in my Lucy Locket before Macpherson has turned back with the aspirins.

'Are you all right?' he says. 'You're looking a bit pasty, laddie.'

I assure him that I am in cracking form, but I am not altogether reassured as I hurry back to Rathbone. Maybe all this chava is taking it out of me – or rather, taking too much out of me. Thank goodness that my feelings for Caroline are on an ethereal plane as opposed to one of the crutch-bombing variety.

Mrs Rathbone's little boy is not in a good mood when I get back to him. 'You've been a hell of a long time,' he says. 'What have you got?'

'These will sort you out in no time, sir,' I say. 'Take three to start off with and another two before each meal or after relieving yourself.'

'Relieving myself?' says Rathbone. 'I've never heard of that.'

‘Perhaps you know it by a different name, sir,’ I suggest. ‘Having a Tom Tit or a gypsy’s kiss, possibly. I believe that in some circles it’s known as pointing Percy at the porcelain.’

‘I know what relieving yourself means, you cretin!’ snarls Rathbone. ‘I was referring to the business of taking two pills afterwards. Are you sure you’ve got it right?’

‘Now you come to mention it, sir. I think it may have been three.’

‘They’re green,’ says Rathbone. ‘I’ve never seen green aspirins.’

‘It’s a new formulation,’ I say. ‘You mustn’t drink or drive a ship after taking them.’

‘You seem to know a lot about them,’ grunts Rathbone.

‘Doctor Macpherson was very enthusiastic,’ I say. ‘He said they’d have you on your feet in no time.’

‘Get me a glass of water,’ says Rathbone. ‘Three, you said, didn’t you?’

‘Or four to be on the safe side,’ I say.

I scamper out of the cabin the moment he has sloshed them down his hairy goat and set to bulling up his uniform. It doesn’t quite do justice to my power-packed shoulders but you can’t have everything. Sid comes in as I am imparting a razor-sharp crease to the trousers and it is clear from the expression on his face that he is either deep in thought or has just banged his nut on the ventilation shaft.

‘It’s not going to be easy, but I think I can do it,’ he says.

‘You mean, unblock the khazi?’ I say. ‘I wouldn’t try while we’re moored beside Wafer Thin Mintoff’s yacht.’

‘I was referring to the crane,’ says Sid. ‘I’ve been watching the bloke working it. We’ll wait till darkness and then slide back the covers on the hold. I’ll work the crane and you tie a rope round Margaret and Harold. Give two tugs and—'

'Hang on a minute!' I say. 'I don't want to sound unco-operative, Sid, but I may be going ashore this evening. Anyhow, where am I going to get a rope from?'

'Use the strap from one of the trunks she hasn't eaten,' says Sid. 'Come on, Timmo. Don't let me down now. If Pervis finds them he'll make them walk the plank.'

Frankly, I feel like selling tickets for the execution but, stupid berk that I am, I allow myself to be talked into helping Sid. 'It's amazing, Timmo,' he keeps saying. 'But that camel really cares for me.'

Everybody knows that camels don't care for anybody but I let Sid cling on to his dream and borrow his clean Dicky Dirt before he realises what is happening. Rathbone's whistle is all ready to leap into and all I have to do is make sure that its owner is not in a fit state to do the leaping. I wait until seven o'clock and then speed round to his cabin hoping for the best – or worst as far as Rathbone is concerned. When I get there, my rival is lying on the bed looking as if you only needed to wave a fag paper in front of his mush to blow him on to the floor. 'Just passing, sir,' I say.

Rathbone winces as if my choice of words caused him pain. 'I'm not going to be able to go to this thrash tonight,' he groans. 'You'd better get round to the Rankins' cabin and tell them.'

'Oh dear, sir,' I say. 'That is bad luck. Miss Rankin will be upset. What time was she expecting you?'

'Half past eight,' croaks Rathbone. 'Oh! Ooooh! Oh no, not again!!' And he slides off the bed and staggers towards the corridor. Oh dear, if he was not such a Charley 'Arst-ard I might experience a pang of guilt. 'Tell her I'm frightfully sorry but I've got some kind of tummy bug,' he says, quickening his stride.

'Keep taking the tablets,' I call after him.

Right! Now for the transformation scene. Time for the ugly duckling to swan off with the princess. I grab hold of the invitation card which Rathbone has thoughtfully left lying on the table and accelerate back to my cabin. I was hoping to get Sid's business out of the way before I picked up Caroline but it does not look if there is going to be time. Fortunately the 'apenny dip is emptier than the Irish heat of The Brain of Britain Contest so there is not too much danger of me being spotted in Rathbone's clobber. I will have to explain the situation to Caroline as best I can. She looks the kind of girl who likes animals.

Back in the cabin, Sid is beginning to use phrases like 'synchronise watches' and I sense that he is going into his Colditz phase.

'Right,' he says. 'I've got you some bananas.'

'That's very nice of you,' I say. 'I believe they're a big help in stopping you getting scurvy.'

'They're not for you, you berk!' he snaps. 'They're for Margaret and Harold. While they're munching them, you can get them ready for the crane.'

'Are you sure this is going to work?' I ask him. 'I know you're practically infallible in the mental magic department but it does seem to me that there are a number of loose ends that need tying up.'

'Have you got a better idea, clever sticks?' asks Sid threateningly. 'They're not going to walk up all those flights of stairs. I remember how much trouble it was getting Margaret down.'

'She was in the pudding club, then,' I say. 'She's a bit more manoeuvrable now.'

'That's not a very nice way to talk about it,' scolds Sid. 'In the pudding club! "With camel", please. Anyway, I'm not having little Harold straining himself and that is my last word. What do you think you're doing?'

'I'm changing into Rathbone's uniform,' I tell him. 'I'm taking that Rankin bird to a do at Government House.'

'The lengths you go to to get your end away,' scoffs Sid. 'You'll never get her Alan Whickers off.'

'I am not interested in getting her knickers off,' I say, trying to let my tone of voice indicate the deep contempt I feel for this uncouth remark and its crude method of expression. 'There are other things, you know.'

'You mean tights?' says Sid.

I close my eyes in exasperation. Sid has no soul. 'Higher things.'

'Tit slings?' says Sid. 'Am I getting warm?'

'Sid,' I say. 'I know it's difficult for you to understand, but what I feel for this girl isn't just sex. It's something intangerine. Something it's not easy to put your finger on.'

'You usually have no trouble putting your finger on everything,' says Sid. 'Is it her money? She must have a few bob. You want to be careful, you know. People who marry for money, earn it.'

'It's not the bread,' I say. 'It's something in here.' I tap my jam tart. 'Don't you ever look at something and get the feeling that it has been created especially for you?'

Sid thinks for a moment. 'Yeh,' he says. 'A pint of mild and bitter in a glass without a handle.'

After that I give up. Sid is beyond redemption, as the vicar said when he took him to one side at Jason's christening and started talking about 'our souls'. Sid got the wrong end of the giggle stick and tried to shove him down the font.

It is agreed that Sid will sling his hook over the side of the hold at eight-forty-five and I settle down to make myself lovely for Caroline. The trouble is that when you have a lot of time you always ruin yourself, don't you? There is no real need for me to shave but I put in a new blade – Sid's fortunately – and promptly slash myself like I am trying to achieve a Prussian duelling scar. The blood drips on to my white shirt – all right! I know I should have taken it off first – and when I try and rub it off, the collar starts fraying – typical of the rubbish Sid buys. The last Dicky Dirt he bought fell off a lorry while the bloke was still wearing it. In the end I rub it with toothpaste to get the white back but it doesn't really work – possibly because some stupid prick at the laboratory has put a bloody red streak through it. Honestly, if God had intended Sodium Glutisylicarbomanganate to be in toothpaste he would have put it there in the first place. Then there is the accident with the Brasso. That really chokes me. Bloody tin! They ought to put a dispenser on the top. It is no wonder that it slops all over everything. What really gets up my bracket is that the buttons are staybright anyway. First of all, I hold the uniform under the tap but the water is tepid and that does no good. Then I try rubbing it. Then I hold it under the ventilation duct – the air that comes out of that is hotter than what you get from a 'dry your hands' machine – and shave the fluff off the serge with Sid's razor. By the cringe! It is sharp that razor. Amazing how it goes through the material. Perhaps it is not very good quality. What a shame. I was looking so good until I started trying to look better. Now, what can I do to darken down the material again? Ah yes. Lucky me. Muna has left some of her blue eyeshadow – or maybe it is Sid's, it does not really matter overmuch. That should do the trick.

Ten minutes later, I am looking like a million dollars – well, would you believe a couple of quid and the change from a pound of bananas? I slap on the old titfer and – sod it! How did that bloody Brasso get in there? All over my barnet and down to my swallow and sigh. Very unattractive it looks too. Typical! I start off with a couple of hours to kill and now I am running out of time. I stick my nut under the tap and give the inside of the hat a good slosh round. My hair was looking decidedly fanciable as well. Now I look like a Yorkshire terrier that has been caught in a rain storm. I run an old folks at home through my barnet and use a towel to soak up some of the surplus moisture round the area of my rocks and boulders. Now for the hat again. It is twenty-five to nine but I must get the angle right. That is all the difference between the Duke of Edinburgh and the bloke who takes your fare on the 49 bus at Clapham Junction – apart from his colour, of course. I snatch the titfer on to my thatch and – knickers! I have forgotten to empty the water out after rinsing it. What a carve up! I only need Mr Rankin to open the door of his cabin and I will be right up Tom Tit Creek without a paddle.

Fortunately, contact with a host of gleaming Richard the Thirds is spared me because it is the fair Caroline who shoves her boat race round the Rory. 'Oh,' she says. 'I was just beginning to – oh!'

'Lieutenant Rathbone's a bit uncle,' I say, giving it to her straight from the pen holder. 'He asked me to step into his canoes.'

'Is that Nicholas?' says Mrs Rankin's toffee-nosed voice from the background. 'Ask him to come in for a sherry.'

I can see Caroline weighing the proposition up and deciding that it is a bad idea. 'We haven't got time, mumsy,' she says, 'don't wait up for me.' She reaches behind her for a stole and closes the door. I don't hang about trying a gold slipper on one of her plates but whip her round the corner smartish.

'What is going on?' she says. 'What did you say about Lieutenant Rathbone?'

'He's not himself,' I say, thinking how lucky he must be. 'It's something he ate.'

'Poor lamb,' she says. 'Hadn't I better go and see him? Isn't there something he would like?'

'He knows where to find it,' I say hurriedly. 'I think it's best to leave him to sleep. That's a smashing dress you've almost got on.'

'Do you like it?' says the light of my life. 'It's something I just threw on.'

'You nearly missed,' I say, giving her a quick flash of my 'rape yer!' wit. 'No, seriously, it's very effective the way it almost, I mean, sort of shows off your-er – you know—'

'You don't think it's too décolletée?'

'I would never say that,' I say truthfully, wondering what she is on about.

'You're looking very smart,' she says. 'I never knew stewards had dress uniforms.' She wrinkles her hooter and sniffs. 'What are you wearing?'

'You mean, my after-shave lotion?'

She nods. 'It smells like Brasso.'

'Yeh, manly, isn't it?' I say. 'It's the new rugged, metallic niff. They've gone off all the old poncy pongs.'

'It's very distinctive,' says Caroline sounding as if she still reckons Aramis. 'Why are we going this way?'

Curses! I was hoping she would not notice. 'There's – er something I must do before we go ashore,' I say casually. 'Got to unload a couple of camels. Won't take a moment.'

'A couple of camels!' Caroline sounds surprised which is no surprise.

'Yes. Always best to do it in the evening when it's cool. Do you like camels? They have some very interesting habits. Most people just think of them as what goes underneath the camel saddles but there's much more to it than that'

'But why you?' asks Caroline.

'I have it away with animals,' I say – 'I mean, I have a way with animals.'

Caroline looks relieved. 'You're a man of many parts, aren't you?' she says. 'How's your Twanky?'

Well, well. You could knock me down with a feather. It is always the quiet ones, isn't it? There am I thinking that this bird is a ringer for one of the Vesta Virgins and she—

'I mean, your Widow Twanky,' she says.

'Oh, of course,' I say. 'The ship's pantomime. I'd forgotten about that. We had to put off rehearsals because the principal boy got shingles.'

'How unpleasant,' says Caroline.

'It was,' I say. 'He borrowed the principal girl's home perm to do it and didn't tell him.'

I leave Caroline looking at me with a puzzled expression on her boat race and throw open the door of the baggage hold. Phew! What a niff. There must be something in those trunks that disagrees with the girls. 'Do you want to wait here?' I say. 'The light's not very good and I'd hate you to—' I pause, wondering how to put it.

'No, I'll come with you. I've never seen a camel at close quarters.'

'Right,' I say. 'Step this way – correction. Step a little bit to the left of this way.'

'Good heavens,' she says. 'What's happened to all the trunks?'

'The camels have had a go at them,' I say. 'Trunks seem to be their staple diet if they can't get staples. Are you worried about—?' I break off when I remember how the Rankins' trunk perished at Southampton station. 'At there we are. Whoah, my proud beauty.'

Margaret does not acknowledge my greeting but rips another two feet of leather off the trunk she is munching. I don't know who supervises her personal freshness programme but they certainly can't have Ministry of Health approval. Harold hovers by Mum's side looking sulky – still, camels always look sulky, don't they?

'Isn't he sweet!' says Caroline. She reaches out a hand to pat Harold and Margaret waves her neck in a 'piss off!' gesture and belches with a pong that makes garlic smell like attar of roses. I look up to the ceiling and am relieved to find that a length of cable with a heavy hook on it is descending through the open hatch. What appears to be the back bumper of a Ferrari is bent over the hook but I imagine that this arrived when Sid was trying to get the hang of the crane and is not meant to be used in the rescue operation.

'Right,' I say. 'I'll just get out my banana and we'll have a go.'

For some reason, this remark seems to disturb Caroline, who takes a swift step backwards when I delve down the front of my trousers. 'Blimey, right down to my knee,' I say. 'Ah, there we are. How do you fancy this, then?'

But neither Margaret nor Harold seem to like bananas and Caroline holds up a restraining hand when I offer her one – it is a bit warm and crushed, I suppose.

'It amazes me that they're not in a crate,' says Caroline. 'Look at all the damage they've done.'

I get the shivers when she says that. The hold looks like a chapter of Hell's Angels have been holding an induction ceremony.

Should Pervis connect Noggett and Lea with this load of pony we could be walking home along the ocean bed.

'Quick!' I say, my voice full of steely purpose. 'Hand us that leather strap. I'll get rid of the nipper while Mum's crunching up that corset.'

It is easy to write about it, but stumbling round that hold with a young camel in your arms is no cup of tea I don't mind telling you. By the time I have got the strap round its belly and given a couple of yanks I am decidedly ruffled, not to mention covered in camel hair from head to foot.

'I always wanted a camel hair coat,' I say with a light laugh.

'You were wonderful,' says Caroline. 'Even when it bit you. I love men who know how to handle animals. I used to have a crush on our vet at home.'

This is good news but I don't have time to dwell on it because Margaret gets her nose out of a trunk and cops an eyeful of junior disappearing through the hatch opening. This seems to distress her more than somewhat because she lets out a piercing bellow closely followed by a louder version of the same thing. 'Ssh!' I say. 'Don't get your knickers in a twist, Margaret. This is only a temporary separation.'

But Margaret is not satisfied and attempts a permanent separation of my hand from the rest of its arm. They are wicked, those hampsteads. They could give you a pastry edge on your elbow.

It occurs to me that the noise could easily attract unwanted visitors and I quickly shut the hold door and drag a packing case against it. 'I want to make sure she doesn't bolt,' I explain, just in case Caroline starts getting worried. The hook swings down into the hold and I remove the piece of ship's rail and look around for Margaret. This is not going to be easy. 'What we need is another pair of corsets,' I say. 'She likes those. You wave them in front of her hooter and I'll get the strap round her.'

'I say, this is tremendous fun,' says Caroline. 'Do you often do things like this?'

'Very often,' I say. 'Here, try her with this binocular case. No sooner have I disappeared under Margaret's belly – and believe me, folks, it is not a place I would recommend for your summer holidays – than there is the sound of someone trying to get into the hold followed by loud banging.

'What's that?' says Caroline.

'That's the signal for us to take a powder,' I tell her. 'Quick! Get on her back.'

'But isn't it dangerous?' she says.

'Not as dangerous as staying here,' I say. 'I'll explain later. Come on! Do you want to go in front of the hump or behind?' I hook the strap on to the hawser and help Caroline on to a packing case. An area of light round the door is getting larger as it is forced open and I can hear Pervis shouting.

'Jump!' We sprawl across Margaret's back and I give a couple of hefty yanks on the cable. After a pause that seems like minutes, the cable tightens and we are jerked into the air. The door bursts open and Margaret bellows into the night. Up, up and away. It is just like Chitty Chitty Bang Bang if you have a vivid imagination.

CHAPTER ELEVEN

In which Timmy, Sid and Caroline attend a soirée at Government House, Malta, and meet Admiral and Louise Quemby of the US Navy. Also in which Timmy and Caroline share something very beautiful.

'Sorry about that,' says Sid.

'That's all right,' I say. 'I've always wondered what the inside of a funnel looked like.'

'Yes,' says Caroline. 'It makes you realise what it must have been like to be a child chimney sweep in the old days.'

'Only they weren't issued with camels, were they?' I say.

'The controls weren't the same as on the one I had when I was a kiddy,' mutters Sid.

'Oh dear,' I say. 'That's the trouble with neuralgia, isn't it?'

'Nostalgia,' says Caroline.

'That too,' I say. 'Look, Sid. You realise you nearly killed us, don't you?'

'I've said I'm sorry,' says Sid. 'I can't go on apologising. You were hardly under the water for any length of time. Anyway, it's washed most of the soot off. You'll soon dry out. The night is balmy.'

'The night is raving bonkers,' I say. 'How do you think we're going to go round to Government House looking like this?'

But when I say that, I reckon without the incredible phlegm and mucus – not to mention the recurrent streak of insanity – that characterise the British upper classes.

They always perk up when you and I would be throwing in the plastic loofah.

'Oh come on!' trills Caroline. 'It would be a tremendous hoot to roll up like this. Don't be such an old stick-in-the-mud, Timothy. We can always pretend we thought it was fancy dress.'

'What a tophole idea, m'dear,' says Sid, who fancies himself as the poor girl's Duke of Bedford – despite the fact that he thinks you're soft if you clean your teeth. 'Have a spiffing time.'

'Oh, you've got to come too!' says Caroline. 'It wouldn't be the same without you.'

'That was what I was hoping,' I say. 'Do we really have to—?'

But it is no good. When we slide off Margaret outside Government House it is Sid who has got the hump. 'Looks a nice place,' he says. 'Reminds me of the facelift of the Worthing Lido.'

'I don't wish to know that,' I say, having a quick sniff of my armpit when I reckon that nobody is looking. 'What are we going to do with these two? If you'd been prepared to lash out for a taxi we could have left them on the quayside.'

'Never,' says Sid. 'How are they going to porridge for themselves down there? If the control of the environment was left in your hands we wouldn't have a duck-billed flat-arse south of Hendon. These creatures have got to live, Timmo.'

'Here, here!' says Caroline. 'I can tell you're a man of feeling, Mr Noggett.'

'Thank you dear young lady,' says Sid. 'I hope to confirm that impression before the night is out.' The way he looks at her as he slides off Margaret you soon get his drift, and the cold wind of memory runs down the length of my hampton. It is the law of the jungle when Sid and his porkel snorkel are concerned and I recall not many moons ago when my love for a bird called Elizabeth perished on the tip of his militant marquis. (See *Confessions of a Window Cleaner* for harrowing details.)

'You still haven't answered my question,' I say. 'What are we going to do with them? I'm not parking them in the gent's.'

'I should hope not,' says Sid. 'That's no way to treat a lady. Let's take them round the back. These places always have big gardens for dishing out the cucumber sandwiches on the Queen's birthday. They should be able to stock up on the herbaceous borders.'

I am not at all averse to this idea for I reckon we may be able to slip into the reception via the french windows. Sub Lieutenant Rathbone's uniform is not looking its best and I don't reckon that the swarthy geezers eyeing us suspiciously from the doorway are going to break out a Union Jack when they get a close range shufti at me. Best to slip into the throng unannounced and hope that everybody is too pissed to notice that the animal magnetism is blunted. So far, the evening has not been one that will live in my memory for ever and, as far as I am concerned, the sooner we get shot of Harold and Margaret the better. It is the Lea-Rankin love tryst that is supposed to be the main feature on this evening's programme.

'Down here, my darlings,' Sid is talking to the camels, of course, and Caroline and I follow him as he leads them round the side of the building. I take her hand and give it a squeeze and to my relief she returns the pressure.

'I say,' she says. 'This is super fun, isn't it?'

'Ripping,' I say. 'I'm looking forward to getting inside, aren't you?'

'Later,' she says. 'Let's get rid of the camels first.'

At those words, my ears prick up and my prick hares up. Has the lady interpreted my innocent remark as a reference to a Friar Tuck in the not too distant future and – even more interestingly – revealed herself as being not averse to the idea? Before I can make further inquiries, Sid pauses on the edge of a wide expanse of lawn surrounded by trees and shrubs and clears his throat.

'This looks like the end of the trail, old timers,' he says. 'I've brought you as far as I can and now's the time to mosey on by yourselves. Somewhere, beyond those rhododendrons is a whole new world awaiting for the imprint of your hooves. Get out there, and perhaps, who knows, one day you'll spare a thought for old Sid Noggett who—'

'All right, John Wayne,' I say. 'Just give them a kick up the khyber and let's get at the booze.'

'How can you talk like that?' hisses Sid. 'Have you no feelings?'

'Precious few after sitting on the back of that thing,' I say. 'Come on! Let's get shot of them. It's getting parky out here.'

To my left, and behind drawn curtains, I can see the outline of a load of people all, presumably, knocking back the tiddly and sharing jokes with each other. That is where I should be at the moment. Charming Caroline out of her mind and underwear – I know, but our relationship can't be completely spiritual in this day and age, can it?

'Oh look,' says the apple of my thigh as Margaret licks Sid's earhole. 'She's kissing him.'

'She's hungry,' I say. 'Come on, Caroline. We've done our bit for Nature Conservancy Year. Let's get amongst it.' I grab her by the Chalk Farm and start making tracks for the french windows.

'Hang on,' says Sid. 'I might as well have a jar while I'm here.'

'You can't come in looking like that,' I tell him.

'What's wrong with the way I look?' says Sid. 'Surely you've seen riding breeches before?'

'There's a difference between riding breeches and pyjamas tucked in a pair of wellingtons!' I say. 'People are going to notice the difference, Sid. Anyway, the camels are coming.'

'Hurrah! Hurrah!' says Sid. 'What made you think of that?'

'I'm not talking about the song, you twit,' I say. 'I'm talking about Harold and Margaret. They're following us.'

This is indeed true and despite my earlier comments on the nature of the beasts, they do seem to have taken a fancy to Sid. Maybe it is his after-shave lotion.

'No, Margaret,' says Sid. 'We say 'bye, 'bye, now. You go make life of your own. One day you meet camel who is right for you and—'

'Don't start that again!' I hiss. I am just about to give Margaret a sharp tap on the hooter when a french window swings open and a decidedly fanciable bird exposes the top two thirds of her knockers to the night air. 'Oh, look, Elmer!' she squeaks. 'Camels! Gee, what a cute idea. I must try one.'

The guy who looms up beside her is wearing naval uniform and more gold rings than Micky Rooney's ex-wives. I don't know how many ribbons he has on his chest but it looks like the haberdashery counter at Woolworths.

'It doesn't look very safe to me, Louise,' he says doubtfully. 'Are these creatures reliable, driver?'

He is talking to Sid who takes a few moments to come to terms with his new role. 'He probably doesn't understand you, Elmer,' says Louise reprovingly. She plucks at Sid's sleeve before pointing to her sit-feature and then up at Margaret. Sid licks his lips and nods vigorously.

Elmer shrugs his shoulders in a 'what the litttle woman wants, the little woman gets' gesture and shoves a couple of notes with large numbers written on them into Sid's hand. 'Just round the spread a couple of times, Akmed. Nothing too energetic, huh?'

'As Allah wills it, so will she be done, offensive,' says Sid.

It occurs to me, as he helps Louise to mount, that he probably means 'effendi' but I don't comment on it. I am too busy watching the way his hand goes up the inside of her skirt as he pushed her on to Margaret's hump. 'Mush, mush!' he says and trots off into the darkness.

'She's game for anything, that one,' says Elmer admiringly.

Just as well, I think to myself. The look in Sid's eye suggests that it might be a bumpy ride once they get past the bougainvillaea.

'I see you fell off a few times,' says Elmer, staring at my uniform. 'Happier on the bridge, huh?'

'E – oh yeh,' I say, getting his drift. 'You in that line of business, are you?'

'Surely it's Admiral Quemby, isn't it?' pipes up Caroline. 'I think you know my father. Do you remember Milton Keynes?'

Admiral Quemby looks puzzled. 'No relation to the poet, is he?'

'No, that's where we used to live. You came down for the pheasant shooting. I'm Caroline Rankin.'

'Of course!' Quemby's face lights up. 'You were the 'lil golden-haired mite with the twelve-bore. My, how you've changed, honey. Tell me, how is your father?' Caroline's old man seems to know everybody, which is surprising when you think what a nasty piece of work he is. Still, I suppose Stalin knew lots of people, too.

The fact that Admiral Quemby and Caroline used to count dead pheasants together is a bit of luck because it makes it easy for us to slip into the reception and start guzzling the booze. There is no sign of Sid or Mrs Quemby which seems to surprise the Admiral but not me. Sid can be lethal in thick shrubbery. I just hope that Margaret does not get jealous. We have arrived at just the right time because most of those present are paralytically Chopin and indifferent to anything else other than the sound of their own voices. The only people who give me the evil eye are the waiters. They are not quite as pissed as everyone else and have not fallen into the easy trap of mistaking me for Prince Charles on an unofficial state visit. Quemby excuses himself to see what has happened to Louise and I steer another vase of Gunga Din past Caroline's pretty lips.

'I really shouldn't have another one,' she says, gulping it down. 'Daddy says I'm a terrible handful after a brace of drinks.' It is always favourite when a bird talks like that because she is really letting you know in her subtle fashion that she is soon not going to be responsible for what she hopes is going to happen to her.

'One more won't do any harm,' I say. 'Anyhow, you're with me.' I expect her to take advantage of this opening and she does so.

'That's what's worrying me!' she says. 'I saw what happened with that American woman.'

I take her arm between my delicate looks and lingers and deliver the famous Lea slow burn. 'You don't think anything like that could happen with us, do you?' I murmur.

'Well – er I know what sailors are like. Mummy told me.'

'I don't think you're as innocent as you pretend to be, Miss Rankin,' I say, lending my voice a touch of the Humphrey Bogarts and throwing in a puckered upper lip for good measure. 'You must have had some experiences with men other than those you heard about from your mother and father.'

'Well,' she says, turning the same colour as her lipstick. 'I've never gone all the way.'

'Just bloomer braille, huh?' I say.

'I don't know what you mean.'

'I mean, somebody's hand getting inside your panties and – you know how you read braille, don't you?'

Caroline shivers and I don't think it is all distaste. 'You're a terrible man!' she says.

'Just normal,' I husk. 'Come on, answer my question.'

It is strange, but the spiritual side of my relationship with Caroline seems to have faded into the background. I find that this often happens after a few drinks. Funny, isn't it? Now, as I look into her eyes I find that I am looking into her knockers and wanting to find out if her dad was right when he said she was a handful.

'I don't see why I should answer your question,' she says 'It's none of your business what I've done with boys.'

'More than one, eh?' I say. 'You're quite a little raver, aren't you?'

In the far corner of the room there is a table covered with goodies and a large white cloth that hangs down to the thickly carpeted floor. It must be quite snug under there.

'Where are you taking me?' says Caroline.

'Pretend you've dropped something,' I say.

'What do you mean?'

'Slip under the table and I'll join you. It's a bit crowded up here.'

'You must be mad!'

'Go on. Nobody's looking. I'll hold your glass.'

Caroline looks round the room and at that moment I know she is actually going to do it. I give her a wink and a nudge and she puts her hand to her throat, gazes down at the floor and drops to her hands and knees. I take a quick shufti at the couple next to me and when I turn back she is gone. I don't hang about but, I ripple down to tie up my shoelace and disappear through the cloth like a sheik entering the tent of his beloved.

'This is stupid!' says Caroline. 'Supposing somebody found us? I should never—'

I silence her rabbit with the impulsive fervour of my rose hips and press her backwards so that she is stretched out on the carpet. At the same moment, my forceful fingers speed up the inside of her leg and rendezvous at the entrance to her banger hangar.

'What are you doing?' she says.

It is a mystery to me why women bother to say things like that when they know bloody well what you are doing. I suppose they feel that they must say something. I don't answer her but whip my mit inside her panties so fast that I nearly sprain my wrist. The muff fluff puff-scuffs the palm of my hand and Percy's erectile potential approaches maximum elevation. It was very handy, the place I made a slit in Rathbone's trousers, because it means that I don't have to use the zipper. Percy lurches out of the ruptured serge like the creature from the black lagoon and I catch a glimpse of him gleaming evilly in the light reflected from the polished toecaps just a foot or two away. I know that there are chava artists who fancy a bit of in and out when there are lots of people about and I can see the appeal of the sport. The danger of discovery does add a spice of excitement.

'What are you trying to do?' Caroline does persist, doesn't she? I would have thought it was pretty obvious, myself. The Terrible Ten are fighting each other for the honour of being the first digit into Furry Gulch and an excitable forefinger has struggled ahead of its fellows and plunged into the velvet void. Huum. If this lady is a virgin then my grandma can suck a lifebelt like a throat lozenge. Either that or Caroline came out of her mum doing the splits.

'You're right,' I murmur. 'Oh dear, I so wanted to make love to you, too.'

'What do you mean?' she says. The note of unease is just what I want to hear.

'Well,' I wheeze. 'You said you'd never throttled a gopher and you were right. How can I thrust my crude pork banana in where angels fear to park their goloshes? Damn it all, there is a code.' I ease forward the brutal magnificence of my rigid pramrod so she realises what she could be missing.

To my relief, her fingers close round it like it is lucky dip time at a stingy orphanage. 'Oh,' she gasps. 'Oh! What are you doing to me? Oh!!' Her voice goes all wild and woolly at the edges and it is obvious that she is resorting to the old 'get on with it and I will pretend that I was somewhere else at the time' ploy. No wonder she thinks she is a virgin.

Some men might reach out from beneath the table to see if their restless fingers could make contact with a chocolate eclair, but not Clapham's favourite son. Pausing only to crack my nut on the underside of the table so hard that five paper doylies flutter to the floor, I whip her knicks down to her ankles and play the Moonlight Sonata on her snatch at the same time. It is done with a digital dexterity that Arthur Rubinstein would envy and the maestro would cream his jeans when he saw the liquid grace with which I station myself in front of the lady's pulsating pussy. She gives a last meaningless mumble and then succumbs to the entry of my demented dilly-duffer. Once you get inside her it is like stepping on a mouse-trap. SNAP! There is less chance of escaping than of Margaret Thatcher wearing her hair in pigtails. For a girl who has never had it she gives a bleeding good imitation of a tornado getting under a groundsheet.

Before I really like to think about it, I realise that my nuts are coming to the boil. I just hope it doesn't sound as loud from above the table. Caroline stretches out a hand and – too late! – I see that she has grasped the tablecloth. She gives a deafening screech and then pulls down three blancmanges, an ash tray and fourteen sausage rolls. Oh dear, what a shame it had to end like this.

CHAPTER TWELVE

In which Sid becomes involved in an unsavoury incident in the grounds of Government House and withdraws hurriedly.

'Is she often taken like that?' says the ambassador's wife.

'I doubt it,' I say. 'I mean, I don't really know.'

Caroline is having the meringue filling wiped off the back of her dress and playing along with the general impression that she flaked out and rolled under the table where I started giving her the kiss of life – I know it sounds a bit far-fetched but these people are so pissed they would believe anything.

'Hey, lootenant. I'd like a word with you.' A worried looking Quemby has pushed through the crowd of gawpers and appeared at my shoulder. 'I can't find Louise. Can you remember where that Arab guy took you?'

For a moment, he has lost me and then I recall that he thought my slightly dishevelled appearance was caused by falling off Margaret. Oh dear, my fears regarding the deadly El Sid were obviously justified. I had better get out there before there is further unpleasantness.

'Er – yeh, I think so,' I say. 'If you wait here, I'll have a decco.' Unfortunately, Quemby has other ideas and as I wave an unacknowledged farewell to Caroline and steer my noble form through the french windows he is sticking closer to me than a starving Elastoplast.

'I think we went round the path,' I say. 'You go that way and shout if you see anything.'

I wait until he has disappeared into the gloom and make a dive for the darkest, thickest bit of shrubbery I can find.

I am not disappointed. Hardly have I parted the privet than I hear a familiar drawl.

'Oh Sidi! That was really peachy. What is it about you Arabs?'

'It is nothing, oh bloater's bottom.'

'I know that. I guess it must be the way you handle it.'

'Sid!' I shout, leaping forward to warn the shit of the desert. 'Fold your hampton and silently steal away. Her old man is looking for you!'

Sid has really staked himself out a goody this time and I am treating myself to a buckshee goggle at the fast disentangling limbs when I hear a sound like a herd of thirsty water buffalo crashing through the bushes. However, experience tells me that it is not a herd of thirsty water buffalo.

'Louise! What the hell!!'

'It's all right,' I say. 'I can explain nothing.'

But Quemby does not appear to be interested in a lack of explanations. He pushes me aside and makes a dive for Sid. Since my brother-in-law has just succeeded in raising his trousers to thigh level he is in a vulnerable position and I am glad that it is sufficiently dark to prevent me from seeing the colour of the bloodstains. I am just beginning to close my eyes so as to shut out the distressing spectacle of Sid becoming a number of different people, when there is a loud braying noise and Margaret appears from the bushes. Pausing only to spit out half a sundial, she rears up and catches Quemby a cracking blow in the chest with her front hooves. The Admiral stumbles backwards into a flower bed and Sid starts loading Louise Quemby on to Margaret.

'Sid!' I squeak. 'What do you think you're doing!?'

But there is no reply. Before you can shout 'Hi, ho,

Silvo, away!', Sid has scrambled up behind Louise and they are drumming across the croquet lawn like you expect to see the credits supered across them when they hit the skyline.

I would not mind so much if Harold did not fart before he ran after them.

CHAPTER THIRTEEN

In which Timmy gets taken for a ride and bumps into some of his old shipmates.

'A really lovely 'lil lady, lootenant.'

'Yeh,' I say. He doesn't half go on, old Admiral Quemby. The table of his blooming great cabin is littered with photographs of wifey taken from yesterday back to when she was an extra half inch on her mum's waistline.

'Help yourself to another bourbon.' Quemby pours himself half a glassful and pushes the bottle over to me. Blimey! Is that all there is left? I could understand it if it wasn't the second bottle we had opened since we got back to the ship.

'I pay for her to come out for a second honeymoon and this is what happens. And with an Arab camel driver. Can you beat it?'

'I think I better had,' I say, looking at my watch. 'I was supposed to be on board an hour ago.'

'You stay put,' says Quemby, jabbing his finger at me and spilling half his bourbon on the floor. 'I'll get the helicopter to take you back when we've finished our chat. I think you're an un'erstan'ing young man. I need someone to talk to at a moment like this. Eighteen years. That's a long time. It hits you kinda hard after eighteen years.'

'It must do,' I say. 'Still, I wouldn't worry too much. She'll be back.'

'I don't think I want her back,' says Quemby, shaking his head slowly. 'I don't think I ever want to see her again.' He picks up one of the photographs and a tear runs down his cheek. Oh my gawd! How am I going to get away? I must have been here for hours.

At that moment, an invisible telephone rings. Quemby unhooks it from beneath the desk and, with difficulty, guides it to his earhole. 'Yup,' he says. 'Uh huh, yep, yup. I'll be right up.' He guides the telephone back with a shaky hand and turns to me. 'We're pulling out,' he says. 'Let's jaw some more on the bridge.'

'Pulling out?!' I screech. 'You mean, putting to sea?'

'The same,' says Quemby rising unsteadily to his feet. 'You know, she wore my pin after our first date.'

I imagine that it must have been because there was something wrong with the lady's knicker elastic but I don't say anything. I am copping a view of the harbour lights sliding past the porthole. 'Where are you going?' I ask.

'I can't tell you,' says Quemby. 'You might be a communist spy. Com'n, let's hit the bridge.'

I thought bridges were places where blokes like Jack Hawkins wearing polo neck sweaters and duffle coats, squinted through binoculars and were brought cups of tea by unable seamen who looked like Richard Attenborough but this is much posher. It is completely enclosed so that the seagulls can't shit on you and there is no sign of one of those wheels with skittles all the way round it. Everybody salutes as we roll up and Admiral Quemby steadies himself with difficulty. 'Very well, lootenant,' he says. 'I am going to bestow upon you a privilege accorded to no other officer in the British Royal Navy. I am going to let you take the helm.'

'That's very nice of you, sir,' I say. 'I've always wanted a—' I break off when I suddenly realise what he is getting at. 'Steer the ship?' I say.

'I thought you'd like to get the feel of her,' says Quemby.

'You limies haven't got anything quite like this.'

'I don't know if I ought to,' I say. 'I mean, it being a Yank – I mean, an American boat and all that.'

'If I say so, you can do it,' says Quemby. 'Just past this cruise ship.'

'You mean, the one with the geezer and the two camels and the bird going up the gang plank?' I say.

'What?' Quemby's mince pies probe the grey early morning light and he starts to bellow orders into a receiver. Immediately, bells start ringing and the ship changes direction so violently that I am thrown against one of the bulkheads.

'Oh no!' I say. 'You mustn't! You can't ram them!'

Before me, the *Tern* looms up like twenty-five elephants standing on top of each other.

Something tells me that my nautical career is nearing a close.

BEN HALL

Frank Clune

Australia in 1860. A time of exploration, gold rushes, gun fights and the cruel tyranny of the cat over transportees. A time when gangs of outlawed robbers and escaped convicts roamed the outback, bushrangers achieved immortalisation in song and legend. Men like Donahoo, Frank the Darkie and bold Ben Hall – men who'd rather die in a bloody battle with the traps than perish in irons.

This is the true story of those pioneer days, of the men and women who took the challenge of their new, wild, unmapped continent and tamed it.

'Ben Hall' is now a major television series from BBC/ABC, created and produced by Neil McCallum.

THE SWEENEY

Ian Kennedy Martin

Jack Regan is one of the Heavy Mob.
He's also a loner, intolerant of red tape and insubordinate to his superiors.
And he just happens to be the best detective in Scotland Yard's crack Flying Squad.

When Regan receives orders to co-operate with Lieutenant Ewing, over from America to trace a cop killer, Regan is pursuing his own case and ignores them. But he soon discovers that Ewing is as tough as he is – and a dangerous clash of personalities develops. As the two cases begin to merge into a sinister and violent network of IRA provos and murderers, the two men close in for the kill . . .

Ian Kennedy Martin is the creator of Thames Television's enormously popular TV series, starring John Thaw.

THE ULTRA SECRET

F. W. Winterbotham

'The greatest British Intelligence coup of the Second World War has never been told till now'
Daily Mail

For thirty-five years the expert team of cryptanalysts who worked at Bletchley Park have kept the secret of how, with the help of a Polish defector, British Intelligence obtained a precise copy of the highly secret and complex German coding machine known as Enigma, and then broke the coding system to intercept all top-grade German military signals. Group-Captain Winterbotham was the man in charge of security and communication of this information. Now he is free to tell the story of that amazing coup and what it uncovered.

'A story as bizarre as anything in spy fiction . . . the book adds a new dimension to the history of World War II'
New York Times

'Military historians, like the general reader, will be astonished by this book . . . Group-Captain Winterbotham cannot be too highly commended'
The Listener

'Superbly told'
Daily Express